THE LILAC GIRL

BY

RALPH HENRY BARBOUR

RALPH HENRY BARBOUR

I.

Two men were sitting beside a camp-fire at Saddle Pass, a shallow notch in the lower end of the Sangre de Cristo Range in southern Colorado. Although it was the middle of June and summer had come to the valleys below, up here in the mountains the evenings were still chill, and the warmth of the crackling fire felt grateful to tired bodies. Daylight yet held, although it was fast deepening toward dusk. The sun had been gone some little time behind the purple grandeur of Sierra Blanca, but eastward the snowy tips of the Spanish Peaks were still flushed with the afterglow.

Nearby three ragged burros were cropping the scanty growth. Behind them the sharp elbow of the mountain ascended, scarred and furrowed and littered with rocky debris. Before them the hill sloped for a few rods and levelled into a narrow plateau, across which, eastward and westward, the railway, tired from its long twisting climb up the mountain, seemed to pause for a moment and gasp for breath before beginning its descent. Beyond the tracks a fringe of stunted trees held precarious foothold on the lower slope of a smaller peak, which reared its bare cone against the evening sky. There were no buildings at Saddle Pass save a snow-shed which began where the rails slipped downward toward the east and, dropping from sight, followed for a quarter of a mile around the long face of the mountain. It was very still up here on the Pass, so still that when the Western Slope Limited, two hours and more late at Eagle Cliff, whistled for the tunnel four miles below the sound came echoing about them startlingly clear.

"Train coming up from the west," said the elder of the two men. "Must be the Limited." The other nodded as he drained the last drop in his tin cup and looked speculatively at the battered coffee pot.

"Any more of the Arbuckle nectar, Ed?" he asked.

"Not a drop, but I can make some."

"No, I've had enough, I reckon. That's the trouble with dining late, Ed; you have too much appetite."

"We'll have to get some more grub before long," was the reply, "or it'll be appetite and nothing else with us. I can eat bacon with the next man, but I don't want to feast on it six days running. What we need, Wade, is variety."

"And plenty of it," sighed the other, stretching his tired legs and finding a new position. "The fact is, even after this banquet I feel a little hollow."

"Same here, but I figure we'd better go a little short till we get nearer town. We ought to strike Bosa Grande to-morrow night."

"Why not hop the train and go down to Aroya? We can find some real grub there."

"Couldn't get back before to-morrow afternoon. What's the good of wasting a whole day?"

"Looks to me like we'd wasted about twenty of them already, Ed."

Craig made no reply. He fished a corn-cob pipe and a little sack of tobacco from his pocket and began to fill the bowl. Wade watched for a moment in silence. Then, with a protesting groan, he rolled over until he could get at his own pipe. Craig drew an ember from the edge of the fire with calloused fingers, held it to his bowl and passed it on to Wade. Then with grunts of contentment they settled back against the sagging canvas of their tent and puffed wreaths of acrid smoke into the twilight.

The shadows were creeping up the mountain side. Overhead the wide sweep of sky began to glitter with white stars. A little chill breeze sprang up in the west and fanned the fire, sending a fairy shower of tiny lemon-yellow sparks into the air. And borne on the breeze came a hoarse pounding and drumming that grew momentarily louder and reverberated from wall to wall. The ground trembled and the grazing burros lifted their shaggy heads inquiringly.

"She's almost up," said Wade. Craig nodded and replaced his pipe between his teeth. The noise became multisonous. With the clangor of the pounding wheels came the stertorous gasping of the engines, the creak and clatter of protesting metal. The uproar filled the pass deafeningly.

"She's making hard work of it," shouted Craig.

"Probably a heavy train," Wade answered.

Then a path of pale light swept around the elbow of the mountain and the wheezing, puffing monsters reached the head of the grade. The watchers could almost hear the sighs of relief from the two big mountain-climbers as they found the level track beneath them. Their breathing grew easier, quieter as they clanged slowly across the pass a few rods below the camp. The burros, having satisfied their curiosity, went back to supper. The firemen in the cab windows raised their hands in greeting and the campers waved back. Behind the engines came a baggage and express car, then a day coach, a diner and a sleeper. Slower and slower moved the train and finally, with a rasping of brakes and the hissing of released steam, it stopped.

"What's up?" asked Wade.

"Hot-box on the diner; see it?"

"Yes, and smell it. Let's go down."

But Craig shook his head lazily, and Wade, cinching his loosened belt, limped with aching legs down the slope. The trainmen were already pulling the smouldering, evil-smelling waste from the box, and after watching a minute he loitered along the track beside the car. Several of the shades were raised and the sight of the gleaming white napery and silver brought a wistful gleam to his eyes. But there was worse to come. At the last table a belated diner was still eating. He was a large man with a double chin, under which he had tucked a corner of his napkin. He ate leisurely, but with gusto.

"Hot roast beef," groaned Wade, "and asparagus and little green beans! Oh Lord!"

He suddenly felt very empty, and mechanically tightened his leather belt another inch. It came over him all at once that he was frightfully hungry. For the last two days he and his partner had been travelling on short rations, and to-day they had been on the go since before sun-up. For a moment the wild idea came to him of jumping on the train and riding down to Aroya just so he could take a seat in the dining-car and eat his fill.

"They wouldn't make much out of me at a dollar a throw," he reflected, with a grin. But it wouldn't be fair to Craig, and he abandoned the idea in the next breath. He couldn't stand there any longer, though, and see that man eat. He addressed himself to the closed window before he turned away.

"I hope it chokes you," he muttered, venomously.

Some of the passengers had descended from the day coach to stretch their limbs, and with a desire to avoid them Wade walked toward the rear of the train. Daylight dies hard up here in the mountains, but at last twilight held the world, a clear, starlit twilight. Overhead the vault of heaven was hung with deep blue velvet, pricked out with a million diamonds. Up the slope the camp-fire glowed ruddily. In the west the smouldering sunset embers had cooled to ashes of dove-gray and steel, against which Sierra Blanca crouched, a grim, black giant. Wade had reached the observation platform at the end of the sleeping-car. With a tired sigh he turned toward the slope and the beckoning fire. But the sound of a closing door brought his head around and the fire no longer beckoned.

On the platform, one hand on the knob of the car door as though meditating retreat, stood the straight, slim figure of a girl. She wore a light skirt and a white waist, and a bunch of flowers drooped from her breast. Her head was uncovered and the soft brown hair waved lustrously away from a face of ivory. The eyes that looked down into his reflected the stars in their depths, the gently-parted mouth was like a vivid red rosebud in the dusk. To Wade she seemed the very Spirit of Twilight, white and slim and ethereal, and so suddenly had the apparition sprung into his vision that he was startled and bewildered. For a long moment their looks held. Then, somewhat faintly,

"Why have we stopped?" she asked.

So unreal had she looked that his heart pounded with relief when she spoke.

"There's a hot-box," he answered, in the tones of one repeating a lesson learned. His eyes devoured her face hungrily.

"Oh!" said the girl, softly. "Then—then you aren't a robber, are you?" Wade merely shook his head. "I heard noises, and then—when I opened the door—and saw you standing there—." The first alarm was yielding to curiosity. She glanced at the scarred and stained hand which grasped the brass railing, and from there to the pleasant, eager, sunburnt face under the upturned brim of the battered sombrero. "No, I see you're not that," she went on reflectively. "Are you a miner?"

"No, only a prospector. We're camped up there." He tilted his head toward the slope without moving his gaze.

"Oh," said the girl. Perhaps she found that steady, unwinking regard of his disconcerting, for she turned her head away slightly so that her eyes were hidden from him. But the soft profile of the young face stood clear against the darkening sky, and Wade gazed enravished.

"You are looking for gold?" she asked.

"Yes."

"And—have you found it?"

"No."

"Oh, I'm so sorry!" There was sympathy in the voice and in the look she turned upon him, and the boy's heart sang rapturously. Perhaps weariness and hunger and the girl's radiant twilit beauty combined to make him light-headed; otherwise how account for his behavior? Or perhaps starlight as well as moonlight may affect the brain; the theory is at least plausible. Or perhaps no excuse is needed for him save that he was twenty-three, and a Southerner! He leaned against the railing and laughed softly and exultantly.

"I've found no gold," he said, "but I don't care about that now. For I've found to-night what is a thousand times better!"

"Better than—than gold!" she faltered, trying to meet his gaze. "Why, what—"

"The girl I love!" he whispered up to her.

She gasped, and the hand on the knob began to turn slowly. Even in the twilight he could see the swift blood staining the ivory of her cheek. His eyes found hers and held them.

"What is your name?" he asked, softly, imperatively.

Oh, surely there is some quality, some magic power in mountain starlight undreamed of in our philosophy, for,

"Evelyn," whispered the girl, her wide eyes on his and a strange wonder on her face.

"Evelyn!" he echoed radiantly. "Evelyn! Evelyn what?"

"Walton," answered the girl obediently. He nodded his head and murmured the name half aloud to his memory.

"Evelyn Walton. And you live in God's country?"

"In New York." Her breath came fast and one hand crept to her breast where the flowers drooped.

"I'll remember," he said, "and some day—soon—I'll come for you. I love you, girl. Don't forget."

There was a quick, impatient blast from the engine. The wheels creaked against the rails. The train moved forward.

"Good night," he said. His hand reached over the railing and one of hers fell into it. For a moment it lay hidden there, warm and tremulous. Then his fingers released it and it fled to join its fellow at her breast.

"Good night—dear," he said again. "Remember!"

Then he dropped from the step. There was a long piercing wail of the whistle that was smothered as the engine entered the snow-shed. The girl on the platform stood motionless a moment. Then one of her hands dropped from her breast, and with it came a faded spray of purple lilac. She stepped quickly to the rail and tossed it back into the twilight. Wade sprang forward, snatched it from the track and pressed it to his lips. When the last car dipped into the mouth of the snow-shed he was still standing there, gazing after, his hat in hand, a straight, lithe figure against the starlit sky.

II.

Well down in the southeastern corner of New Hampshire, some twenty miles inland from the sea, lies Eden Village. Whether the first settlers added the word Village to differentiate it from the garden of the same name I can't say. Perhaps when the place first found a name, over two hundred years ago, it was Eden, plain and simple. Existence there proving conclusively the dissimilarity between it and the original Eden, the New England conscience made itself heard in Town Meeting, and insisted on the addition of the qualifying word Village, lest they appear to be practising deception toward the world at large. But this is only a theory. True it is, however, that while Stepping and Tottingham and Little Maynard and all the other settlements around are content to exist without explanatory suffixes, Eden maintains and is everywhere accorded the right to be known as Eden Village. Even as far away as Redding, a good eight miles distant, where you leave the Boston train, Eden's prerogative is known and respected.

Wade Herrick discovered this when, five years after our first glimpse of him, he stepped from the express at Redding, and, bag in hand, crossed the station platform and addressed himself to a wise-looking, freckle-faced youth of fourteen occupying the front seat of a rickety carryall.

"How far is it to Eden, son?" asked Wade.

"You mean Eden Village?" responded the boy, leisurely.

"I suppose so. Are there two Edens around here?"

"Nope; just Eden Village."

"Well, where is that, how far is it, and how do I get there?"

"About eight miles," answered the boy. "I kin take you there."

Wade viewed the discouraged-looking, flea-bitten gray horse dubiously. "Are you sure?" he asked. "Have you ever driven that horse eight miles in one day?"

"Well, I guess! There ain't a better horse in town than he is."

"How long will it take?"

"Oh, about an hour; hour an' a half; two hours—"

"Hold on! That's enough. This isn't exactly a sight-seeing expedition, son. We'll compromise on an hour and a half; what do you say?"

The boy examined the prospective passenger silently. Then he looked at the horse. Then he cocked an eye at the sun. Finally he nodded his head.

"All right," he said. Wade deposited his satchel in the carriage and referred to an address written on the back of a letter.

"Now, where does Mr. Rufus Lightener do business?"

"Over there at the bank."

"Good. And where can I get something to eat?"

"Stand up or sit down?"

"Well, preferably 'sit down.'"

"Railroad Hotel. Back there about a block. Dinner, fifty cents."

"I certainly am glad I found you," said Wade. "I don't know what I'd have done in this great city without your assistance. Now you take me over to the bank. After that we'll pay a visit to the hotel. You'd better get something to eat yourself while I'm partaking of that half-dollar banquet."

An hour later the journey began. Wade, fairly comfortable on the back seat of the carryall, smoked his after-dinner pipe. The month was June, there had been recent rains and the winding, dipping country road presented new beauties to the eyes at every stage. Wade, fresh from the mountains of Colorado, revelled in the softer and gentler loveliness about him. The lush, level meadow, the soft contour of the distant hills, the ever-present murmur and sparkle of running water delighted him even while they brought homesick memories of his own native Virginia. It was a relief to get away from the towering mountains, the eternal blue of unclouded skies, the parched, arid miles of unclothed mesa, the clang and rattle of ore cars and the incessant grinding of quartz mills. Yes, it was decidedly pleasant to have a whole summer—if he wanted it—in which to go where he liked, do what he liked. One might do much worse, he reflected, than find some such spot as this and idle to one's heart's content. There would be trout, as like as not, in that stony brook back there; sunfish, probably, in that lazy stream crossing the open meadow yonder. It would be jolly to try one's luck on a day like this; jolly to lie back on the green bank with a rod beside one and watch the big white clouds sail across the wide blue of the sky. It would seem almost like being a boy again!

Presently, when, after passing through the sleepy village of Tottingham, the road crossed a shallow stream, Wade bade the boy drive through it.

"Don't have to," replied unimaginative fourteen. "There's a bridge."

"I know there is," answered Wade, "but my doctor has forbidden bridges. Drive through the water. I want to hear it gurgle against the wheels."

He closed his eyes, expectantly content, and so did not see the alarmed look which the boy shot at him. The horse splashed gingerly into the stream, the wheels grated musically over the little stones, and the water lapped and gurgled about the spokes. Wade leaned back with closed eyes and nodded approvingly. "Just the same," he murmured. "It might be the ford below Major Dabney's. This is surely God's own country again."

Further on they rattled through the quiet streets of East Tottingham, a typical New England village built around a square, elm-shaded common. It was all as Ed had described it; the white church with its tall spire lost behind the high branches, the Town Hall guarded by an ancient black cannon, the white houses, the green blinds, the lilac hedges, the toppling hitching-post before each gate. Tottingham Center succeeded East Tottingham and they eventually reached Eden Village twenty minutes behind schedule.

It was difficult to say where country left off and village began, but after passing the second modest white residence Wade believed he could safely consider himself within the corporate limits. Before him stretched a wide road lined with elms. So closely were they planted that their far-reaching branches formed a veritable roof overhead, through which at this time of day the sunlight barely trickled. They were sturdy trees, many of them larger in the trunk than any hogs-head, and doubtless some of them were almost as old as the village itself. The cool green-shadowed road circled slightly, so that as they travelled along it the vista always terminated in a wall of green, flecked at intervals with a gleam of white where the sun-bathed front of some house peeked through. Wade viewed the quaint old place with interest, for here Ed had lived when a boy, and many a story of Eden Village had Wade listened to.

The houses were set, usually, close to the street, with sometimes a wooden fence, sometimes a hedge of lilacs before them. But more often yard and sidewalk fraternized. Flowers were not numerous; undoubtedly the elms threw too much shade to allow of successful floriculture. But there were lilacs still in bloom, lavender and white, and their perfume stirred memories. The houses in Eden Village were not crowded; for the first quarter of a mile they passed hardly more than a dozen. After that, although they became more neighborly, each held itself well aloof. Then came a small church with a disproportionately tall spire, a watering trough, the Town Hall, and "Prout's Store, Zenas Prout 2nd, Proprietor." Here the gray sidled up to the ancient hitching-post. The boy tossed the reins over the dashboard and jumped out. "You don't need to hold him," he said reassuringly. Presently he was back. "It's further up the street," he announced. "But he says there ain't anybody livin' there an' the house is locked up."

"I've got the key," answered Wade. "Go ahead."

They went on along the leafy nave. Now and then a road or grass-grown lane started off from the main highway and wandered back toward the meadow-lands. Presently the street straightened out, the elms presented thinner ranks, houses stood farther apart. Then the street divided to enclose a narrow strip of common adorned with a flagpole greatly in need of a new coat of white paint. The elms dwindled away and an occasional maple dotted the common with shade. The driver guided the patient gray to the left and, near the centre of the common, drew up in front of a little white house, which, like the picket fence in front of it, the flagstaff on the common, and so many other things in Eden Village, seemed to be patiently awaiting the painter.

Inside the fence, thrusting its branches out between the pickets, ran a head-high hedge of lilac bushes, so that, unless you stood directly in front of the gate, all you saw of the first story were the tops of the front door and the close-shuttered windows. Between house and hedge there was the remains of a tiny formal garden. Rows of box, winter-killed in spots, circled and angled about grass-grown spaces which had once been flower-beds. The dozen feet of path from gate to steps was paved with crumbling red bricks, moss-stained and weed-embroidered. The front door had side-lights hidden by narrow, green blinds and a fan-light above. Wade drew forth the key entrusted to him by the agent and tried to fit it to the lock. But although he struggled with it for several moments it refused stubbornly to have anything to do with the keyhole.

"There's a side door around there," advised the boy from the carryall. "Maybe it's the key to it."

"Maybe it is the key to it," responded Wade, wiping the perspiration from his forehead. He pushed his way past the drooping branches of an overgrown syringa, tripped over a box-bush, and passed around the left of the house, following the remains of a path which led him to a door in an ell. Back here there were gnarled apple and pear and cherry trees, a tropical clump of rhubarb, and traces of what had evidently been at one time a kitchen garden. Old-fashioned perennials blossomed here and there; lupins and Sweet Williams and other sturdy things which had resisted the encroachment of the grass. The key fitted readily, scraped back, and the narrow door swung inward.

Gloom and mustiness were his first reward, but as his eyes became accustomed to the darkness he saw that he was in the kitchen. There was the sink with a hand-pump on one side and a drain-board on the other. Here a table, spread with figured yellow oil-cloth; a range, chairs, corner-cupboard, a silent, staring clock. His steps beat lonesomely on the floor. A door, reached by a single step, led to the front of the house. He pushed it open and groped his way up and in, across to the nearest window. When the blinds were thrust aside he found himself confronted by a long mahogany sideboard whose top still held an array of Sheffield platters, covered dishes, candlesticks. Save for the dust which lay heavily on every surface and eddied across the sunlight, there was nothing to suggest desertion. Wade could fancy that the owner had stepped out of doors for the moment or had gone upstairs. He found himself listening for the sound of footsteps overhead or on the staircase or in the darkened hall. But the only sounds were faint sighs and crepitations doubtless attributable to the air from the open windows stirring through the long-closed house, but which Wade, letting his fancy stray, chose to believe came from the Ghosts of Things Past. He pictured them out there in the hall, peering through the crevice of the half-open door at the intruder with little, sad, troubled faces. He could almost hear them whispering amongst themselves. He felt a little shiver go over him, and threw back his shoulders and laughed softly at his foolishness.

But the feeling that he was an intruder, a trespasser, remained with him as he passed from room to room, throwing open windows and blinds, and now and then sneezing as the impalpable dust tickled his nostrils. In the sitting-room, as in every other apartment, everything looked as though the occupant had passed out of the room but a moment before. Wade's face grew grave and tender as he looked about him. On the sewing machine a shallow basket held sewing materials and a few pairs of coarse woollen stockings, neatly rolled. The poker was laid straight along the ledge of the big "base-burner" in the corner. A table with a green cloth stood in front of a window and bore a few magazines dated almost ten years before. A set of walnut book-shelves held a few sober-clad volumes, Bulfinch's "Age of Fable," "Webster's Dictionary," Parker's "Aids to English Composition," Horace's "Odes" in Latin, "The Singer's Own Book," "Henry Esmond" and "Vanity Fair," "A Chance Acquaintance," two cook-books, a number of yellow-covered "Farmer's Almanacs," and "A Guide to the City of Boston." A sewing-stand supported a huge family Bible. The walls were papered in brown and a brown ingrain carpet covered the floor. There was a couch under the side window and a few upholstered chairs were scattered about. Now that the windows were open and the warm sunlight was streaming in, it was a cosy, shabby, homey little room.

Wade opened the door into the hall. Perhaps the Ghosts of Things Past scampered up the winding stairway; at least, they were not to be seen. He found the front-door key in the lock and turned the bolt. When the door swung inward a little thrill touched him. For the first time in his life he was standing on his own doorsill, looking down his own front path and through his own front gate!

In every man's nature there is the desire for home-owning. It may lie dormant for many years, but sooner or later it will stir and call. Wade heard its voice now, and his heart warmed to it. Fortune had brought him the power to choose his home where he would, and build an abode far finer than this little cottage. And yet this place, which had come to him unexpectedly and through sorrow, seemed suddenly to lay a claim upon him. It was such a pathetic, down-at-heels, likable little house! It seemed to Wade as though it were saying to him: "I'm yours now. Don't turn your back on me. I've been so very, very lonesome for so many years! But now you've come, and you've opened my doors and windows and given me the beautiful sunlight again, and I shall be very happy. Stay with me and love me."

In the carryall the boy was leaning back with his feet on the dasher and whistling softly through his teeth. The gray was nibbling sleepily at the decrepit hitching-post. Wade glanced at his watch, and looked again in surprise. It was later than he had thought. If he meant to get out of Redding that night it was time he thought of starting back. But after a moment of hesitation he turned from the door and went on with his explorations. In the parlor there was light enough from the front door to show him the long formal room with its white marble centre-table adorned with a few gilt-topped books and a spindly lamp, the square piano, the stiff-looking chairs and rockers, the few pictures against the faded gold paper, the white mantel, set with shells and vases and a few photographs, the quaint curving-backed sofa between the side windows. He closed the door again and turned down the hall.

The stairway was narrow and winding, with a mahogany rail set upon white spindles. It was uncarpeted and his feet sounded eerily on the steps. On the floor above doors opened to left and right. The first led into what had evidently been used as a spare bedroom. It was uncarpeted and but scantily furnished. The door of the opposite room was closed. Wade opened it reverently and unconsciously tiptoed to the window. When the sunlight was streaming in he turned and surveyed the apartment with a catch of his breath. It had been Her room. He had never seen her, yet he had heard Ed speak of her so much that it seemed that he must have known her. He tried not to think of the days when, lying there on the old four-post bed with the knowledge of approaching death for company, she had waited and waited for her son to come back to her. Ed had never forgiven himself that, reflected Wade. He had been off in Wyoming at the time, and when he had returned the two telegrams lay one upon the other with a month's dust over them, the one apprising him of his mother's illness and asking him to hurry home, the other tersely announcing her death. Well, she knew all about it now, reflected Wade. Ed had told her long before this.

It was a pleasant little room with its sloping ceilings and cheerful pink paper. The bed was neatly spread with a patchwork quilt, and the blankets and counterpane were folded and piled upon the foot. The old mahogany bureau was just as she had left it, doubtless. The little, knick-knacks still stood upon the brackets, and in the worsted-worked pincushion a gold brooch was sticking.

He closed the window and returned to the floor below. A door under the stairway led from the hall to the kitchen. He crossed the latter and passed out into the yard. Back of the house the ground sloped slightly to a distant stone wall, which apparently marked the limit there of Wade's domain. At one time there had been a fence between the orchard and the meadow beyond, but now only an occasional crumbling post remained. Trees had grown up here and there in the meadow, a few young maples, a patch of locusts, and some straggling sumacs. Birds sang in the trees, and once, when he listened, Wade thought he could hear the tinkling of a brook.

Toward the centre of the village his ground ran only to a matter of ten or twelve yards from the kitchen door. There was just room for the little garden between house and fence. On that side his nearest neighbor was distant the width of several untenanted lots. On the other side, however, there was more space. There were some shade-trees here, and around one of them, an ancient elm, ran a wooden seat, much carved and lettered. The boundary here was a continuation of the lilac hedge which fronted the street, and in it was an arched gate leading to the next yard. But from the gate all Wade could discern was the end of a white house and a corner of a brick chimney some forty yards distant; trees and shrubbery hid more of his neighbor's estate.

Wade returned to the front of the house, hands in his pockets, a tune on his lips. He had taken his valise from the back of the carryall before the driver, who was half asleep, discovered his presence. He blinked and dropped his feet from the dashboard.

"You all ready?" he asked.

Wade shook his head.

"I've changed my mind," he said. "I'm going to stay awhile."

III.

That was a stirring afternoon in Eden Village. Wade's advent was like the dropping of a stone into the centre of a quiet pool. Prout's Store was the centre of the pool, and it was there that the splash and upheaval occurred, and from there the waves of commotion circled and spread to the farthest margins. By supper time it was known from one length of Main Street to the other that the Craig place was tenanted again. As to who the tenant was rumor was vague and indefinite. But before bedtime even that point was definitely settled, Zenas Prout 2nd having kept the store open a full half-hour later than usual to accommodate delayed seekers after knowledge.

It was a rather stirring afternoon for Wade, too. First there was a visit to the store in the carryall for the purchase of supplies. Mr. Prout, who combined the duties of merchant with those of postmaster and express agent, was filling out a requisition for postal supplies when Wade entered. Poking his pen behind his ear, he stepped out from behind the narrow screen of lock-boxes and greeted the visitor.

"Afternoon, sir. You found the house all right?"

"Yes, thanks." Wade drew forth a pencil and tore off a piece of wrapping paper.

"Sort of out of repairs, of course, seem' it ain't been lived in for most ten years, not since Mrs. Craig died. Was you considerin' purchasin', sir?"

"Er—no." Wade was writing rapidly on the brown paper. "The fact is, Mr. Prout, I own the Craig house now."

"You don't say?" exclaimed the store-keeper in genuine surprise. "You ain't—surely you ain't Ed Craig?"

"No, my name's Herrick. Ed was a good friend of mine. We were partners in a mining enterprise in Colorado. Ed died almost a year ago now; typhoid."

"I want to know! Well, well! So Ed Craig's gone, has he? I remember him when he was 'bout so high. Used to come down here an' I'd set him up on the counter right where you be now, Mr. Herring, and give him a stick of candy. I recollect he always wanted the kind with the pink stripes on it. An' he's dead, you say? We often wondered what had become of Ed. Folks thought it kind of queer he didn't come home the time his mother died."

"He was away and didn't learn of her illness until it was too late," said Wade. "He felt mighty badly about that, Mr. Prout, and I wish you'd let the people here know how it happened. Not that it matters much to Ed now, but he was the best friend I ever had, and I don't want folks who used to know him to think he deliberately stayed away that time."

"That's so, sir. An' I'm glad to hear the truth of it. Ed didn't seem to me when I knew him the sort of feller to do a thing like that. Folks'll be glad to know about it, Mr. Herring."

"Herrick, please. Now just look over that list and check off what you can let me have, will you? I'm going to stay awhile, and so I will have to get in a few provisions."

Mr. Prout ran his eye down the list dubiously, checking now and then. When he laid it down and pushed it across the counter his tone was apologetic.

"Ain't a great deal there I can sell you, Mr. Herrick. I'm kind of out of some things. I guess I can get most of 'em for you, though, if you ain't got to have 'em right away."

Wade looked at the slip.

"You put up what you've got," he said, "and I'll send over to Tottingham Center for the rest."

"Don't believe you'll get 'em all there," commented Mr. Prout. "Things like bacon in jars an' canned mushrooms there ain't much call for around here."

But Wade was busy revising his list, and made no comment. Presently he went out and despatched the boy to the Center. When he returned to the store Mr. Prout was weighing out sugar.

"So you come into the Craig place, Mr. Herrick. I suppose you bought it."

"No, Ed left it to me in his will. Wanted me to come on here and have a look at it and see that it was all right. He was very fond of that place. So I came. And—well, it's a pleasant place, Mr. Prout, and it's a pretty country you have around here, and so I reckon I'll stay awhile and camp out in the cottage."

"Going to do your own cooking?" asked Mr. Prout.

"Have to, I reckon. It won't be the first time, though."

"Guess you wouldn't have any trouble findin' some one to come in an' do for you, if you wanted they should," said Mr. Prout. "There's my gal, now. She's only fifteen, but she's capable an' can cook pretty tolerable well. Course you know your business best, Mr. Herrick, but—"

"Send her over in the morning," said Wade, promptly. "Is there a mail out of here to-night?"

"Five o'clock."

"Then let me have a sheet of paper and a stamped envelope, if you please. I'll write down to Boston and have them send my trunk up."

He met but few persons on his way back to the cottage, but many a curious gaze followed him from behind curtained windows, and, since the ripples had not yet widened, he left many excited discussions in his wake. Back in the cottage he threw off coat and vest, lighted his pipe and set to work. First of all, up went the parlor windows and shades. But a dubious examination of that apartment was sufficient. If he should ever really live here the parlor could be made habitable, but for the present its demands were too many. He closed the windows again and abandoned the room to its musty solitude. From the spare room upstairs he brought bed and bedding and placed it in the sitting room. It required some ingenuity to convert the latter apartment into a bedroom, but the difficulty was at last solved by relegating the sewing machine to the parlor and moving the couch. When the bed was made Wade went out to the kitchen and looked over the situation there. Closet and cup-board displayed more dishes and utensils than he would have known what to do with. He tried the pump and after a moment's vigorous work was rewarded with a rushing stream of ice-cold water that tasted pure and fresh. Then he looked for fuel. The lean-to shed, built behind the kitchen, was locked, and, after a fruitless search for the key, he pried off the hasp with a screw-driver. The shed held the accumulated rubbish of many years, but Wade didn't examine it. Fuel was what he wanted and he found plenty of it. There was a pile of old shingles and several feet of maple and hickory neatly stowed against the back wall. Near at hand was a chopping-block, the axe still leaning against it. There was a saw-horse, too, and a saw hung above it on a nail. But there was no wood cut in stove size, and so Wade swung the door wide open to let in light, and set to work with the saw and axe. It felt good to get his muscles into play again and he was soon whistling merrily. Fifteen minutes later he was building a fire in the kitchen stove. It was too early for supper, but the iron kettle looked very lonely without any steam curling from its impertinent spout. After he had solved the secrets of the perplexing drafts, and ascertained by the simple expedient of placing a sooty finger in it that the water was really getting warm, he washed his hands at the sink and returned to the sitting-room to don vest and coat. He had done that and was ruminantly filling his pipe when something drew his gaze to one of the side windows. The pipe fell to the floor and the tobacco trailed across the carpet.

For a moment, for just the tiny space of time which it took his heart to charge madly up into his throat, turn over and race back again, the open casement framed the shoulders and face of a woman. There were greens and blues in the background, and sunlight everywhere, and a blue shadow fell athwart the sill. The picture glared with light and color, but for that brief fragment of time Wade's eyes, half-blinded by the dazzlement, looked into the woman's. His widened with wonder and dawning recognition; hers—but the vision passed. The frame was empty again.

Wade passed a hand over his eyes, blinked and asked himself startledly what it meant. Had he dreamed? He gazed dazedly from the fallen pipe to the empty window. The sunlight dazzled and hurt, and he closed his eyes for an instant. And in that instant another vision came.... It was twilight on Saddle Pass.... Two starlit eyes looked wonderingly down into his. The mouth beneath was like a crimson bud with parted petals.... A slim, warm hand was in his and his heart danced on his lips.... The slender form lessened and softened in the tender darkness and became only a pale blur far down the track, and he was standing alone under the cold white stars, with a spray of lilac against his mouth.

He opened his eyes with a shiver. It was uncanny. All that had been five years ago, five years filled to the brim with work and struggle and final attainment, all making for forgetfulness. The thing was utterly absurd and impossible! His senses had tricked him! The light had blinded his eyes and imagination had done the rest! And yet—

He strode to the window and looked out. The garden was empty and still. Only, under the window, at the edge of the path, lay a spray of purple lilac.

IV.

"Eh? Yes? What is it?"

Wade sat up in bed and stared stupidly about him. In Heaven's name where was he? And what was the noise that had awakened him? There it was again!

Rat, tat, tat, tat!

Was he still asleep? What was this room? The stove looked dimly familiar, and there were his clothes over the back of a green rep rocker. But where—Then memory routed sleep and he sank back onto the pillow with a sigh of relief. It was all right. He remembered now. He was in his own cottage in Eden Village, he had had a fine long sleep and felt ready for—

Rat, tat, tat, tat—TAT!

"Hello! What is it? Who is it? Why in thunder don't you—"

"Please, sir, it's me."

The reply came faintly through the dining room. Some one was knocking at the kitchen door. The apologetic tones sounded feminine, however, and Wade was in no costume to receive lady visitors. He looked desperately around for his dressing-gown and remembered that it was in his trunk and that his trunk still reposed in the porter's room of a Boston hotel.

"Who—who is 'me'?" he called.

"Zephania."

Zephania! Who in thunder was Zephania?

"I'm very sorry, Miss Zephania, but I'm not dressed yet. If you wouldn't mind calling again in, say, half an hour—"

"Please, sir, I'll wait."

"Oh, well—er—was there something you wanted?"

"Please, sir, I've come to do for you."

To do for him! Wade clasped his knees with his arms and frowned perplexedly at the big stove. It was distinctly threatening. He wondered how she intended to accomplish her awful purpose. Perhaps she had stopped in the woodshed and secured the axe. To do for him! Then he laughed and sprang out of bed. It was Zenas Prout's girl, and she had come to get his breakfast.

"Zephania!" he called.

"Yes, sir?" It sounded as though she were sitting on the back doorstep.

"The door is unlocked. Come in. You'll find things to eat on the table and things to cook with in the closets. I'll be dressed in a few minutes."

He heard the door open as he closed his own portal, and in a moment a stove-lid fell clanging to the floor. After that Zephania's presence in the house was never for a moment in doubt. Rattle-bang went the poker, clicketty-click went the shaker, and triumphant over all rose Zephania's shrill young voice:

"'O Beulah land, sweet Beulah land,
As on thy highest mount I stand;
I look away across the sea,
Where mansions are prepared for me.'"

"She has a cheerful presence," muttered Wade. "I wonder if she does that all the time."

But Zephania's vocal efforts were forgotten for the moment in the annoying discovery that he had neglected to provide washing accommodations. He had intended using the kitchen sink for ablutions, but with Zephania in possession of that apartment it was out of the question. It was evident that if he meant to wash in the kitchen he would have to get up earlier. What time of day was it, anyhow? He looked at his watch and whistled.

"Twenty minutes of seven!" he ejaculated. "This won't do. I guess I'd better get my own breakfasts. If there's one thing a chap wants to do in vacation it's sleep late."

He raised the shades and flung open the front windows. On the lilac hedge a bird was poised singing his heart out. Wade watched him in admiration and wondered what kind of a bird he was. To Wade a bird was a bird as long as it was neither a buzzard nor a crow.

"You're not a buzzard," he told the songster, "nor a crow. You have a gray breast and brown body and a black cap on your head. Wonder who you are. Guess you're a sparrow. I believe I'll get a book telling about birds. They're interesting little devils. Look at him put his head back! Just as though he meant to crack things wide open. By Jove! I have it! Your name's Zephania!"

A baker's cart ambled by beyond the hedge, the driver leaning around the corner of the vehicle to regard the cottage curiously. Out on the common a bay horse, his halter-rope dragging under his feet, cropped the lush grass.

"You're happy," murmured Wade. "The bird's happy. Zephania's happy. This must be a happy village." He pondered a moment, gazing contentedly about the cosy sunlit room. Then, "And I'm happy myself," he added with conviction. And to prove it he began to whistle merrily while he finished dressing. Presently there was a knock on the dining-room door.

"Yes?" responded Wade.

"Please, sir, what will you have for breakfast?" Being by this time decently dressed, Wade opened the door.

"Hello!" he said.

"Good morning," answered Zephania.

If he had not been informed that her age was fifteen Wade would have supposed Zephania's years to be not over a baker's dozen. She was a round-faced, smiling-visaged, black-haired, black-eyed, ruddy-cheeked little mite who simply oozed cheerfulness and energy. She wore a shapeless pink cotton dress which reached almost to her ankles, and over that a blue-checked apron which nearly trailed on the floor. Her sleeves were rolled elbow-high and one little thin hand clutched a dish-cloth as a badge of office. Wade stared dubiously at Zephania and Zephania smiled brightly back.

"Look here, my child," said Wade, "how old are you, anyway?"

"Fifteen in March, sir."

"Next March?"

"No, sir, last."

"You don't look it."

"No, sir, folks say I'm small for my age," agreed Zephania, cheerfully.

"I agree with them. Do you think you're strong enough to do the work here?"

"Oh, yes, sir. This is a very easy house to look after."

"Well," said Wade, hesitatingly, "you can have a try at it, but it seems to me you're too young to be doing housework."

"I've always done it," replied Zephania, beamingly. "What'll you have for breakfast, sir?"

"Coffee—can you make coffee?"

"Yes, sir, three ways."

"Well, one way will do," said Wade, hurriedly. "And you'll find some eggs there, I believe, and some bread. You might fry the eggs and toast the bread. I guess that will do for this morning."

"Yes, sir, thank you," answered Zephania, politely. "Wouldn't you rather have the eggs poached?"

"Er—why, yes, if you can do it."

"I can cook eggs eleven ways," said Zephania, proudly. "Are you going to eat breakfast in here or in there?" She nodded past Wade at the sitting-room.

"Well, what do you think?"

"It's sunnier in there, sir. I could just clear the end of that table. There's a fine big tray, sir."

"An excellent idea," replied Wade. "I place myself—and my house—in your hands, Zephania."

"Thank you, sir," said Zephania.

Breakfast was prepared that morning to the strains of "Jesus, Lover of My Soul." Wade went out to the kitchen presently to wash hands and face at the sink and dry them on a roller towel, which Zephania whisked before him as if by magic. Watching her for a minute or two dispelled all doubts as to her ability. The way in which she broke the eggs and slipped them into the boiling water was a revelation of dexterity. And all the while she sang on uninterruptedly, joyously, like the gray-breast on the hedge. Wade went out into the garden and breathed in deep breaths of the cool, moist air. The grass and the shrubs were heavy with dew and the morning world was redolent of the perfume exhaled from moist earth and growing things. In the neglected orchard the birds were chattering and piping, and from a nearby field came the excited cawing of crows. It was corn-planting time.

Wade ate his breakfast by the open window. He didn't know in which of the three ways Zephania had prepared his coffee, but it was excellent, and even the condensed milk couldn't spoil it. The eggs were snowy cushions of delight on golden tablets of toast, and the butter was hued like old ivory. Zephania objected to condensed milk, however, and suggested that she be allowed to bring a quart of "real milk" with her when she came in the mornings.

"Of course, you won't need a whole quart, unless you drink it, but, if you like cream in your coffee, it'll be a great deal heavier from a quart than from a pint. We get six cents for milk."

"By all means, let us have a quart," replied Wade, recklessly. "Such good coffee as this, Zephania, deserves the best cream to be had." Zephania blushed with pleasure and beamed down upon him radiantly.

"And maybe, sir, you'd like me to make you some bread?"

"I would. I was about to broach the subject," was the mendacious answer. "Could you do it?"

"Yes, indeed. Why, when they had the church fair over to The Center last winter I sent four loaves, and Mrs. Whitely, that's the minister's wife, sir, said it was just as good as any there."

"I want to know!" said Wade, unconsciously falling into local idiom.

"Yes, sir. I can make two kinds of bread. I'll make the milk bread first, though, and let you try that. Most folks likes milk bread the best. Shall I set some to-night?"

"Set some? Oh, yes, please do."

While she was removing the tray Zephania asked: "Which room would you like to have me clean first, sir?"

"Well, I suppose we ought to clean the whole place up, hadn't we?"

"Oh, yes, sir! Everything's just covered with dust. I never did see such a dirty house. Houses do get that way, though, if they're shut up for a long time. Maybe I'd just better begin at the top and work down?"

"That seems sensible," said Wade. "You could just sort of sweep the dirt down the front stairs and right out of the front door, couldn't you?"

"Oh, no, sir," replied Zephania, with a shocked, pitying expression. "I'd never do that. I'd clean each room separately, sir; sweep and wash up the floors and around the mop-board and—"

"Whatever way you think best," interrupted Wade. "I leave it all to you, Zephania, and I'm sure it will be done beautifully."

"Thank you, sir. Mother says I'm a real smart cleaner. Shall I get some more flowers in this vase, sir? This piece of lilac's dreadfully wilted."

"No, Zephania, just let that remain, please. The fact, is, that—that's a rather particular piece of lilac; something out of the common."

"Out of the common?" echoed Zephania, in faint surprise, surveying as much of the common as she could see through the window. "You don't mean our common?"

"No," answered Wade, gravely, "not our common. That piece of lilac, Zephania, is a clue; at least, I think it is. Do you know what a clue is?"

"Yes, sir. It's something you find that puts you on the trail of the murderer." Zephania eyed the lilac interestedly.

"Well, something of that sort. Only in this case there isn't any murderer."

"A thief?" asked Zephania, eagerly and hopefully.

"Not even a thief," laughed Wade. "Just—just somebody I want very much to find. I suppose, Zephania, you know about every one in the village, don't you?"

"Pretty nearly, I guess."

"Good. Now suppose you tell me something about my neighbors. Every one ought to know about his neighbors, eh?"

"Yes, sir. After you've been here some time, though, you'll know all about them."

"Yes, but the trouble is I don't want to wait that long. Now, for instance, who lives over there on my left; the square white house with the drab blinds?"

"Miss Cousins, sir. She's a maiden lady and has a great deal of money. They say she owns some of the railroad. She plays the organ in church, and—"

"Youngish, is she, with sort of wavy brown hair and—"

"No, sir," Zephania tittered, "Miss Cousins is kind of old and has real gray hair."

"Really? On my other side, then, who's my neighbor there? Or haven't I one?"

"Oh, yes, sir," answered Zephania, eagerly. "That's the Walton house, and that's—"

"The—*what*?" asked Wade, sitting up very suddenly in the green rep rocker.

"The Walton house, sir."

"Oh! Hum! And—er—who lives there, Zephania?"

"Miss Walton and Miss Mullett."

"What's this Miss—Miss Walton like? Is she rather stout with quite black hair, Zephania?"

"Oh, no, Mr. Herring! I guess you saw Mrs. Sampson, the dressmaker. She lives over there across the common, in the little yellowish house with the vines; see?"

"Yes, yes, I see. That's where Miss Sampson lives, eh? Well, well! But we were speaking about Miss Walton, weren't we?"

"Yes, sir. Miss Walton's a young lady and as pretty as—as—" Zephania's words failed her and she looked about apparently in search of a simile.

"Now let's see what you call pretty," said Wade. "What color is her hair?"

"It's brown."

"Oh, well, brown hair isn't uncommon."

"No, sir, but hers is kind of wavy and light and I don't believe she ever has to curl it."

"You don't tell me! And her eyes, now? I suppose they're brown too?"

"Blue, sir. She has beautiful eyes, Mr. Herring, just heavenly! Sometimes I think I'd just give almost anything if my eyes were like hers."

"Really? But you seem to have a very good pair of your own. Don't trouble you, do they?"

"They're black," said Zephania, cheerfully. "Black eyes aren't pretty."

"Oh, I wouldn't go as far as that," murmured Wade, politely.

"No, sir, but Miss Walton's are just as blue as—as the sky up there between those two little white clouds. She's awfully pretty, Mr. Herring."

"Complexion dark, I suppose."

"No, sir, not dark at all. It's real light. Some folks say she's too pale, but I don't think so. And sometimes she has just lots of pink in her cheeks, like —like a doll I have at home. Folks that think she's too pale ought to have seen her yesterday afternoon."

"Why is that?'"

"'Cause she was just pink all over," answered Zephania. "I took some eggs up to her house and just when I was coming out she came up on the porch. She looked like; she'd been running and her face was just as pink as—as that lamp-mat!"

The object in question was an excruciating magenta, but Wade let it pass.

"Yesterday was rather a warm day for running, too," observed Wade.

"Yes, sir, and I don't see what made her run, because she had been in the garden. Maybe a bee or a wasp—"

"How did you know she had been in the garden?"

"Why, 'cause she came from there. She hadn't ought to run like that in hot weather, and I told her so. I said 'Miss Eve'—What, sir?"

"Nothing," answered Wade, poking industriously at the tobacco in the bowl of his pipe. "You were saying—"

"I just told her, 'Miss Eve, you hadn't ought to overheat yourself like that, 'cause if you do you'll have a sunstroke.' There was a man over at the Center last summer who—"

"And what did she say?" asked Wade.

"She said she'd remember and not do it again. And then Miss Mullett came out and I went home."

"Who's Miss Mullett, Zephania?"

"She's Miss Walton's friend. They live there together in the Walton house every summer. Folks say Miss Mullett's very poor and Miss Walton looks after her."

"Young, is she?"

"Not so very. She's kind of middle-aged, I guess. She's real pleasant. Miss Walton thinks a lot of her."

"And they're here only in the summer?"

"Yes, sir. They come in June and stay until September. This is the third summer they've been here. Before that the house was empty for a long, long time; just like this one."

"Very interesting, Zephania. Thank you. Now don't let me keep you from your labors any longer."

"No, sir, but don't you want to hear about any one else?"

"Another time, thanks. We'll do it by degrees. If you tell me too much at once I shan't be able to remember it, you see."

"All right," answered Zephania, cheerfully. "Now I'll wash up the dishes."

After she had gone Wade sat for a long while in the green rep rocker, his eyes on the spray of lilac on the table and his unlighted pipe dangling from his mouth. From the kitchen came a loud clatter of dishes and pans and Zephania's voice raised in song:

"'We shall sleep, but not forever,
There will be a glorious dawn;
We shall meet to part, no, never,
On the resurrection morn!'"

V.

When one has spent six years prospecting and mining in Colorado and the Southwest one has usually ceased to be capable of surprise at any tricks Fate may spring. Nevertheless Wade was forced to wonder at the chain of events which had deposited him here in a green rep rocking chair in Eden Village. That the Western Slope Limited, two hours late and trying to make up time, should have had a hot-box and, perhaps for the first time in months, stopped at the top of Saddle Pass and presented Evelyn Walton to him was one of Fate's simpler vagaries; but that now, after five years, he should find himself beside her nearly two thousand miles from their first place of meeting was something to think about. First event and last were links in a closely-welded chain of circumstance. Looking back, he saw that one had followed the other as logically as night follows day. By a set of quite natural, unforced incidents Fate had achieved the amazing.

Wade no longer had any doubt as to the identity of the person who had looked in upon him through the window yesterday. The marvellous resemblance to the face he remembered so well, the dropped lilac spray were in themselves inconclusive, but the evidence of her name made the case clear and left but one verdict possible. Chance, Fate, Providence, what you will, had brought them together again.

It would, I realize, add interest to a dull narrative to say that Wade's heart beat suffocatingly with passionate longing, and that a wild desire to go to her possessed him. As a matter of fact his heart behaved itself quite normally and he showed no disposition to leave his chair. He was chiefly concerned with wondering whether she had recognized him, whether she even remembered him at all, and, if she did, what she thought of him for the idiotic way in which he had acted. Oh, he had been sincere enough at the moment, but, looked at calmly with the austere eyes of twenty-eight, his behavior on that occasion had been something—well, *fierce*! He groaned at the thought of it and almost wished that Fate had let things alone and spared him a second meeting. Of course there had been extenuating circumstances. She had stepped suddenly into his vision out of the twilight, a veritable vision of love and romance, and his heart, a boy's heart, starved and hungry for those things, had taken fire on the instant. He had—well, he had lost his head, to put it charitably. And after a fashion he had lost his heart as well. For a week he had dreamed of her at night and thought of her by day, had wondered and longed and built air castles. Doubtless, had he seen her again within the next year, the romance would have grown and flourished. But at the end of that first week they had found gold. The intoxication of success succeeded the intoxication of love, and in the busy months that followed the vision of Evelyn Walton's face visited him less and less frequently. At the end of a year she had become a pleasant memory, a memory that never failed to bring a half-sad, half-joyous little throb. That he had never actually forgotten her meant little, when you think how very tiny and unimportant a thing must be to utterly escape memory. He didn't want to forget her, for she represented the only sentimental episode that had come to him since school days. He had been much too busy to seek love affairs, and up in the mountains they don't lie in wait for one. Therefore at twenty-eight Wade Herrick was heart-whole. He wondered with a smile how long he was destined to remain so unless that same meddling Fate removed either him or Evelyn Walton from Eden Village.

Zephania went through the hall singing, on her way upstairs to inaugurate her war of extermination against dirt. Wade roused himself and lighted his pipe. After all, he had done nothing criminal and there were ninety-nine chances in a hundred that the girl wouldn't connect him for a moment with the astounding youth who had made violent love to her for an ecstatic five minutes on the top of Saddle Pass so many years ago. He got up and looked at himself in the old gold-framed mirror above the table.

"My boy," he muttered, "you're quite safe. You used to be fairly good looking then, if I do say it myself. But now look at you! You have day-laborer written all over you! Your hair—I wonder when and why you ever began to part it away down near your left ear. But that's easily changed. Your nose—well, you couldn't alter that much, and it's still fairly straight and respectable. But that scar on the cheek-bone doesn't help your looks a bit, my boy. Still, you mustn't kick about that, I reckon, for if that slice of rock had come along an inch or so farther to the right you'd have been *tuerto* now. Not that your eyes are anything to be stuck up about, though; they're neither brown nor green, nor any other recognized color; just a sort of mixture—like Pedro's *estofados*. Your mouth, now—you always had a homely sort of mouth, too big by far. And you were an idiot to shave off your mustache. You might let it grow again, now that you're where you could have it trimmed once in awhile, but I suppose it would take a month and look like a nail-brush in the meanwhile! And then there's your complexion, you poor ugly *hombre*. I remember when it was like anybody else's and there was pink in the cheeks. Look at it now! It's like a saddle-flap. And your hands!"

He viewed them disdainfully. They were immaculately clean and the nails were well tended, but two years of pick and shovel had broadened them, and at the base of each finger a calloused spot still remained. On the left hand the tip of one finger was missing and another was bent and disfigured. They were honorable scars, these, like the one on his cheek, but he looked at them disgustedly and finally shoved them out of sight in his pockets.

"No, don't you worry about her recognizing you," he said to the reflection in the mirror. "Even if she did she'd be ashamed to own it!"

Wade, however, was over-critical. Whatever might be said of the features individually, collectively they were distinctly pleasing. The impression one received was of a clean, straight-limbed, clear-eyed fellow, who, if he had worked with his hands, had won with his brain. He looked a little older than his twenty-eight years warranted, and a little taller than his scant five-feet-eleven proved. Above all, he appeared healthful, alert, capable, and kindly. He made friends at sight with men, children, and dogs and wore his friendships as easily as he wore his clothes. The West puts an indefinable stamp on a man, and Wade had it. When presently he donned a cloth cap, torn from the confused depths of his valise, and passed out of doors he walked like a man who was used to covering long distances afoot, and with a certain swing of his broad shoulders that suggested a jovial egotism. And as he made his way through the orchard and into the meadow beyond his mind was still busy with Evelyn Walton.

Of course he would meet her sooner or later; he was bound to unless he pulled up stakes and hiked out at once. And he didn't want to do that. He was enjoying a totally new sensation, that of householder. And he liked Eden Village with its big elms and shaded roads, its wide meadows and encircling green hills. It was all new and delightful after the bare, primeval grandeur of the mountains. Besides, and Wade laughed softly to himself, when all was said and done, he really wanted to meet her. The prospect brought a flutter to his heart and a pleasant excitement to his mind. He would probably fall in love with her again, but there was no harm in that since he would be off before the disease could strike in very deep.

He had reached the stone wall dividing his property from the land beyond. At a little distance a brook bubbled along its sunken course. Bushes, ferns, and here and there a small tree lined its banks, and Wade could follow its journeying with his eyes for some distance. He vaulted the wall and crossed to the brook, examining it with the curiosity of a fisherman. It was rather disappointing. He didn't believe any self-respecting fish would deign to inhabit such meagre quarters. But it was a fascinating little stream for all of that, and it sang and purled and had such a jolly good time all to itself that unconsciously Wade fell into step with it, so to speak, and kept it company through the meadow. Swallows darted above him and sparrows took flight before him in mild alarm. Once he disturbed a catbird on her nest and she flew circling about his head, scolding harshly.

What had he been thinking about a moment before? Oh, yes, he had been considering the danger of overdoing the falling in love business. Well, there was a proverb about its being better to have loved and lost than never to have loved at all. Wade agreed with those sentiments. To go head over ears in love with some nice girl like—well, like Evelyn Walton—even if you got turned down was better than nothing. Of course the girl mustn't know. It wasn't a part of his plan to worry her any. He was quite certain that if he was careful she needn't even guess his sentiments. Perhaps—well, what if it was nonsense? A fellow could think nonsense if he wanted to, couldn't he, on a day like this? Perhaps she might care for him enough to marry him! There wasn't any reason why he shouldn't marry. He had plenty of money and would have more; he could give the woman that married him about as much as the next man. She could have a house in New York if she wanted it! And servants and—and motors and—all the things a woman usually wants. Of course he didn't want to be married for his money, but—well, he wondered whether it would help if he managed to convey the idea that he was pretty well off, that he owned more than a controlling interest in one of the richest gold mines in Colorado. Undoubtedly there were girls who would jump at the chance to marry the principal owner of a mine like the —

He stopped with a gasp.

Great Scott! she mustn't hear the name of that mine! At least, not unless things turned out as they never could turn out. He groaned. He would have to watch himself every minute when he was with her or he would be blurting it out!

He found himself confronted by a fence, beyond which a wooded hill sloped upward. Should he return the way he had come, or—no, he could commit trespass on somebody's wheat field and so in all probability reach the highway. Five minutes later he found himself on the road and started back towards the cottage. He rather hoped that Miss Walton would not be on her front porch as he went by. He wasn't quite ready yet to show himself. It was a good ten minutes' walk to the end of the common, but he was so busy with his thoughts that he paid little attention to time or distance. He only came to himself when he suddenly found the lilac hedge beside him and the gate hospitably open. He walked up the steps, dimly conscious that his cottage looked this morning far less disreputable than it had seemed yesterday, and tried the front door. He didn't remember whether he had locked it last night. But evidently he had not, for it swung open and he found himself staring blankly into a pair of very lovely and much surprised blue eyes.

VI.

Time passed.

Somewhere about the house a canary twittered softly. Evelyn Walton, arrested on the sitting room threshold, a fold of the light portière clasped in one hand, gazed at the intruder. Wade, frozen to immobility just inside the door, one hand still grasping the knob, gazed at the girl. His mind was a blank. His lips moved mechanically, but no words issued from them. It seemed to him that whole minutes had passed, although in reality the old-fashioned clock at the end of the hall had ticked not more than thrice. He felt the color surging into his face, and at last sheer desperation loosened his tongue.

"Is there anything I can do—" he began.

But at the very same moment Evelyn Walton's power of speech returned likewise, and—

"You wished to see—some one?" she inquired.

As they spoke absolutely together neither heard the other's question and each silently awaited an answer.

"*Tick ... tock*" said the old clock, sleepily.

Wade's gaze wandered. He wondered whether it would be unforgivable to dash quickly out and slam the door behind him. But in the next breath escape was forgotten and he was looking about him in sheer amazement. Here was his hallway, but no longer empty. A shield-backed chair stood beside the parlor door. A settle ran along the wall beyond. A pink-cheeked moon leered at him from the top of a tall clock. Bewilderedly he looked toward the sitting-room. There, too, everything was changed. The floor was painted gray. Rugs took the place of carpet. Gauzy lace curtains hung at the windows. A canary in a gilt cage sung above an open window. Oh, plainly he was bewitched or the world was topsy-turvy! The look he turned on the girl was so helpless, so entreating that her face, which had begun to set coldly, softened instantly. The hand clasping the curtain fold fell to her side and she took a step toward him.

"Can I help you?" she asked, kindly.

Wade passed a hand over his eyes.

"I don't know," he murmured. "Will you please tell me where I am?"

"You're in my house. I am Miss Walton."

"Your house? Then—then where is mine, please?" he asked, helplessly.

"Just beyond here; the next one."

"Oh!" he said. He sought for words with which to explain the situation, but found none. He backed out, tripped slightly over the sill and found himself on the top step. He dared one more look into the girl's amused and sympathetic face and then turned and fled precipitately. At the gate he brushed against some one, muttered an apology, and plunged through. Evelyn Walton, following his course of flight from the doorway, laughed softly. Miss Caroline Mullett, standing on tiptoe in the middle of the path, strove to see over the hedge, and, failing, turned to the girl with breathless curiosity.

"Why, Eve, who was that?"

"He didn't leave his card, dear," replied Eve, with a gurgle of suppressed laughter, "but there is every reason to believe that his name is Herrick."

"The gentleman who has taken the next house? And what did he want? He seemed in such a hurry, and so very much excited! You don't think, do you, that he is going to have a sunstroke? His face was extremely congested."

"No, dear," replied Eve, as she followed Miss Mullett into the sitting-room, "I don't think he's in danger of sunstroke. You're getting to be quite as bad as Zephania on that subject. The fact is, dear, that the ensanguined condition of Mr. Herrick's face was due to his having mistaken our humble abode for his."

"My dear! How embarrassing!"

"So he seemed to think," laughed Evelyn.

"But I can quite understand it," continued Miss Mullett, laying aside her hat and smoothing down her hair. Miss Mullett's hair was somewhat of the shade of beech leaves in fall and was not as thick as it had once been. She wore it parted in the middle and combed straight down over the tips of her ears. Such severe framing emphasized the gentleness of her face. "You know yourself, Eve dear, that the first summer we were here we often found ourselves entering the wrong gate. The houses are as much alike as two peas."

"I know. But, oh, Carrie, if you could have seen his expression when it dawned on him that he was in the wrong house! It's too bad to laugh at him, but I just have to."

"I hope you didn't laugh while he was here," said Miss Mullett, anxiously.

"I'm afraid I did—just a little," replied Eve, contritely. "But I don't think he saw it. He was too—too bewildered and horrified, and terribly embarrassed. I really pitied him. I don't think I ought to pity him, either, for he gave me quite a fright when he opened the front door and walked in just as though he'd come to murder us all."

"Poor man!" sighed Miss Mullett. "He must be feeling awfully about it. And—and didn't you think him exceedingly nice looking? So big and—and manly!"

"Manly?" laughed Eve. "He looked to me more like a very small boy discovered in the preserve closet!"

"Of course, but I'm afraid you were a little—oh, the least little bit unfeeling, dear."

"Perhaps I was," owned Eve, thoughtfully. "I shouldn't want him to think me—impolite."

"No indeed! Do you think he will call?"

"After this morning? My dear Carrie, did he look to you like a man coming to call?"

"But in a day or two, perhaps? Don't you think that it is possibly our duty to convey to him in some delicate manner that he—that we—that his mistake was quite natural—"

"We might put a personal in the Tottingham *Courier*. 'If the gentleman who inadvertently called at The Cedars on Tuesday morning will return, no questions will be asked and all will be forgiven.' How would that do?"

"I'm afraid he would never see the paper unless we lent him our copy," replied Miss Mullett, with a smile. "But surely we might convey by our manner when meeting him on the street that we would be pleased to make his acquaintance?"

"Why, Caroline Mullett!" gasped Eve, in mock astonishment. "What kind of behavior is that for two respectable maiden ladies?"

"My dear, I'm an old maid, I know, but you're not. And if you think for a moment that I'm going to sit here and twiddle my thumbs while there's a nice-looking bachelor in the next house, you're very much mistaken. Dear knows, Eve, I love Eden Village from end to end, but I never heard of an Eden yet that wasn't better for having a man in it!"

"You're right," sighed Eve. "Do you realize, Carrie, that the only eligible man we know here is Doctor Crimmins? And he's old enough to be father to both of us."

"The Doctor plays a very good hand of cribbage," replied Miss Mullett, approvingly. And then triumphantly: "I have it, dear!"

"What?"

"The Doctor shall call on Mr. Herrick and bring him to see us!"

"Splendid!" laughed Eve. "And he will never know that we schemed and intrigued to get him. Carrie, I don't see how, with your ability, you ever missed marriage."

"I never have missed it," replied Miss Mullett, with a sniff. She took up her hat and started toward the hall. At the door she turned and seemed about to speak, but evidently thought better of it and disappeared. Eve smiled. And then Miss Mullett's plain, sweet little face peered around the corner of the door, and—

"Much," she whispered.

VII.

When Wade came to himself he discovered that he was standing with folded arms staring blankly at the Declaration of Independence which, framed in walnut and gilt, adorned the wall of the sitting-room. How long he had been standing there he didn't know. He swung around in sudden uneasiness and examined the room carefully. Then he gave a deep sigh of relief. It was all right this time; this was his own house! He sank into the green rocker and mechanically began to fill his pipe. From the floor above came the swish of the broom and Zephania's voice raised in joyful song:

"'I was a wand'ring sheep, I did not love the fold;
I did not love my Shepherd's voice, I would not be controlled.
I was a wayward child, I did not love my home;
I did not love my Father's voice, I loved afar to roam.'"

Wade lighted his pipe, and when he had filled the adjacent atmosphere with blue smoke he groaned. After that he gazed for a long time at his hands, turning them this way and that as though he had never really noticed them before. Then he laughed shortly a laugh seemingly quite devoid of amusement, and got up to wander aimlessly about the room. At last he caught a glimpse of himself in the mirror and walked over to it, and glared fiercely at the reflection for a full round minute. Twice he opened his mouth, only to close it again without a sound. At length, however, the right words came to him. He looked himself witheringly in the eyes.

"You blundering, God-forsaken ass!" he enunciated.

That seemed to cheer him up quite a bit, for he turned away from the mirror with a less hopeless expression on his face and began to unpack his valise and distribute the contents about the room. Later he borrowed some of Zephania's hot water from the singing kettle and shaved himself. No matter to what depths of degradation a man may fall, shaving invariably raises him again to a fair level of self-respect. He ate luncheon with a good appetite, and then wandered down to Prout's Store, ostensibly to ask if his trunk had arrived, but in reality to satisfy a craving for human intercourse. The trunk had not come, Mr. Prout informed him, but, as Wade couldn't well expect it before the morning, he wasn't disappointed. He purchased one of Mr. Prout's best cigars—price one nickel—and sat himself on the counter.

"Yes," said Mr. Prout, "them two houses is a good deal alike. In fact I guess they're just alike. Anyway, old Colonel Selden Phelps built 'em alike, an' I guess they ain't been much changed. I recollect my mother tellin' how the old Colonel had them two houses built. The Colonel lived over near Redding and folks used to say he was land-crazy. Every cent the Colonel would get hold of he'd up an' buy another tract of land with it. Owned more land hereabouts than you could find on the county map, and they say he never had enough to eat in the house from one year's end to t'other. Family half starved most of the time, so they used to tell. The boy, Nathan, he up an' said he couldn't stand it; said he might's well be a Roman Catholic, because then he would be certain of a full meal once in awhile, but as it was every day was fast day. So he run away down to Boston an' became a sailor. The Colonel never saw him again, because he was lost at sea on his second voyage. That just left the two girls, Mary and Evelyn. My mother used to say that every one pitied them two girls mightily. Always looked thin and peaked, they did, while as for Mrs. Phelps, why, folks said she just starved to death. Anyway, she died soon after Nathan was drowned. Just to show how pesky mean the old Colonel was, Mr. Herrick, they tell how one night the women folks was sewing in the sittin'-room. Seems they was workin' on some mighty particular duds and Mrs. Phelps had lighted an extra candle; the Colonel never would allow a lamp in his house. Well, there they was sittin' with the two candles burnin' when in stomps the Colonel. 'Hey,' says he, blowin' out one of the candles, 'what's all this blaze of light? Want to ruin your eyes?'

"Folks liked the Colonel, too, spite of his meanness. He was a great church man, an' more'n half supported the Baptist church over there. Seemed as if he was willin' to give money to the Lord an' no one else, not even his own family. Mary was the first of the girls to get married, she bein' the eldest. She married George Craig, from over Portsmouth way, an'—"

"Craig? Then she was Ed's mother?" interrupted Wade.

"Yes. About a month after the engagement was given out the Colonel drew up the plans of those two houses. He made the drawin's himself, and then sot down an' figured out just how much they'd cost; so much for stone an' masonry; so much for lumber and carpentry; so much for brick an' so much for paint. Then he went to a carpenter over in Redding an' showed him the plans with the figures writ on 'em an' asked him if he'd put up the houses. The carpenter figured an' said he'd be switched if he'd do it for any such price. So the Colonel he goes to another feller with like results. They say most every carpenter between here an' Portsmouth figured on those houses an' wouldn't have anything to do with them. Then, finally, the Colonel found a man who'd just settled down in Tottingham and opened a shop there. Came from Biddeford, Maine, I believe, and thought he was pretty foxy. 'Well,' he says, 'there ain't any money in it for me at those figures, Colonel, but work's slack an' I'll take the contract.' You see, he thought he could charge a little more here an' there an' make something. But he didn't know the Colonel. Every time he'd talk about things costin' more than he'd thought the Colonel would flash that contract on him. When the houses was finished he sued the Colonel for a matter of four hundred dollars, but there was the contract, plain as day, an' he lost his suit. Just about put him out of business an' he had to move away. The Colonel gave one of the houses to Mary—Mrs. Craig she was by that time—and the other to Evelyn when she married Irv Walton a year afterwards."

"But look here," said Wade. "Do you mean that Ed Craig's mother and Miss Walton's mother were sisters?"

"Yes, Ed and Eve was first cousins."

"Well, I'll be hanged!" sighed Wade. "I never savvied that. What became of Mr. Walton, Ed's uncle?"

"Dead. Irv was what you call a genius, a writer chap. Came of a good family over to Concord, he did, an' had a fine education at Exeter Academy. He an' his wife never lived much at The Cedars—that's what they called their place—but used to come here now and then in the summer. They lived in New York. He had something to do with one of those magazines published down there. Irv Walton was a fine lookin' man, but sort of visionary. Made a lot of money at one time in mines out

West an' then lost it all about four years ago. That sort of preyed on his mind, an' somethin' like a year after that he up an' died."

"And his wife?"

"Oh, she died when Eve was a little girl. An' Ed's mother died about ten years ago. Miss Eve's the last one of the old Colonel's folks."

Wade sat silent for a minute, puffing hard on his cigar and trying to arrange his facts.

"Does she know of Ed's death?" he asked.

"Miss Eve? Oh, I guess so. I told Doctor Crimmins myself last night an' I guess he's been up to The Cedars by this time. I guess Ed's death wouldn't affect her much, though."

"Why is that?"

"Well, the brothers-in-law never got on very well together in the old days, an' far as I know Miss Eve never saw Ed except, perhaps, when they were both babies. Ed went away to school, winters down to Boston, to a school of tech—tech—well, a place where they taught him engineerin' an' minin' an' such. Summers he worked in a mill over to Lansing."

"Is Miss Walton well off?"

"Only tolerable, I guess. She's got that house and what little money was saved out of her father's smash-up."

"Where does she live when she's not here, Mr. Prout?"

"New York. She does some sort of writing work, like her father. Inherited some of his genius, I guess likely."

Later Wade walked leisurely back to the cottage. The afternoon sunlight lay in golden ribbons across the deserted street. Up in the high elms the robins were swaying and singing. An ancient buggy crawled past him and here and there an open window framed a housewife busy with her needle. But save for these signs of life, he reflected, he might be walking through the original Deserted Village. Come to think of it, Craig's Camp was a busy metropolis compared to Eden Village, only—Wade paused in front of his garden hedge and peered pleasurably up into the leafy golden mists above him—only for some reason the absence of human beings didn't make for loneliness here. Nature was more friendly. There was jovial comradeship in every mellow note that floated down to him from the happy songsters up there.

"'The cheerful birds of sundry kind Do sweet music to delight his mind.'"

Wade swung around with a start and found himself looking over the hedge-top into a smiling, ruddy, gold-spectacled countenance.

"Spenser, I think, sir," continued the stranger, "but I'll not he certain. Perhaps you recall the lines?"

"I'm afraid I don't," replied Wade, passing through the gateway.

"No? But like enough the poets aren't as much to a busy, practical man like you, Mr. Herrick, as they are to me. Even I don't find as much time to devote to them as I'd like, however. But I haven't introduced myself nor explained my presence in your garden. My name is Crimmins, Doctor Crimmins."

"Glad to know you, Doctor," replied Wade, as they shook hands. "It was friendly of you to call, sir."

The Doctor tucked his gold-headed cane under his arm and thrust his hands into the pockets of his slate-colored trousers, a proceeding which brought to view the worn satin lining of the old black frock-coat.

"Wait until you know us better, sir, and you'll not speak of it as kindness. Why, 'tis a positive pleasure, a veritable debauch of excitement, Mr. Herrick, to greet a newcomer to our mislaid village! The kindness is on your side, sir, for dropping down upon us like—like—"

"A bolt from the blue," suggested Wade.

"Like a dispensation of Providence, sir."

"That's flattering, Doctor. Won't you come in?"

"Just for a moment." At the sitting-room door the Doctor paused. "Well! well!" he exclaimed, reverently under his breath. "Nothing changed! It's ten years ago since I stood here, Mr. Herrick. Dear me! A fine Christian woman she was, sir. Well! Well! 'Time rolls his ceaseless course.' Bless me, I believe I'm getting old!" And the Doctor turned his twinkling gray eyes on Wade with smiling dismay.

"Try the rocking chair, Doctor Crimmins. Let me take your hat and cane."

"No, no, I'll just lay them here beside me. I see you've chosen the best room for your chamber, sir. You're not one of us, Mr. Herrick, that's evident. Here we make the best room into a parlor, the next into a sitting-room, the next into a spare room and sleep in what's left. We take good care of our souls and let our bodies get along as best they may. You, I take it, are a Southron."

"From Virginia, Doctor, and, although I've been in the West for some six years, I hope I haven't entirely forgotten Southern hospitality. Unfortunately my sideboard isn't stocked yet, and all the hospitality I can offer is here." He indicated his flask.

"H'm," said the Doctor, placing his finger-tips together and eying the temptation over his spectacles. "I believe I've heard that it is an insult to refuse Southern hospitality. But just a moment, Mr. Herrick." He arose and laid a restraining hand on. Wade's arm. "Let's not fly in the face of Providence, sir." He guided his host into the dining-room and softly closed the door, cutting off the view from the front window. Then he drew a chair up to the table and settled himself comfortably. "We are a censorious people, Mr. Herrick."

"As bad as that, is it?" laughed Wade as he placed glasses on the cloth and brought water from the kitchen.

"We are strictly abstemious in Eden Village," replied the Doctor, gravely, "and only drink in dark corners. Your very good health, sir. May your visit to our Edenic solitude prove pleasant."

"To our better acquaintance, Doctor."

"Thank you, sir, thank you. Ha! H'm!" And the Doctor smacked his lips with relish, wiped them carefully on his handkerchief and led the way back to the sitting-room.

"And now, Mr. Herrick, to come to the second object of my call, the first being to extend you a welcome. Zenas—I refer to our worthy Merchant Prince, Mr. Zenas Prout—Zenas informed me last evening that you had been a close friend of Ed Craig's, had, in fact, been in partnership with him in some Western mining-enterprise; that Ed had died and that you had come into his property. That is correct?"

"Quite, sir."

"I brought him into the world. I'm sorry to hear of his death. Well, well! 'Our birth is nothing but our death begun, as tapers waste that instant they take fire.' Young's 'Night Thoughts,' Mr. Herrick. Full of beautiful lines, sir." The Doctor paused a moment while he cleaned his spectacles with a corner of his coat. "Let me see; ah, yes. I wonder if you know that you have next door to you Ed's only surviving near relative?"

"I learned it only an hour ago, Doctor."

"I see. I felt it my duty to inform Miss Walton of her cousin's death and called on her at noon. Miss Walton's parents and Ed's were not intimate when the two were children; some silly misunderstanding in regard to a division of old Colonel Phelps's property after he died. As it turned out they might have spared themselves the quarrel, for a later will was afterwards found leaving his entire estate to churches and schools. Well, I was going to say that Ed's death was not much of a grief to Miss

Walton because she had really never known him, but, nevertheless, she would naturally wish to hear the particulars. I came to suggest that you should give me the honor of allowing me to present you to Miss Walton, Mr. Herrick."

"I shall be very glad to meet her," replied Wade, "and tell her all I can about Ed. We were very close friends for several years and a finer chap never breathed."

"I'm delighted to hear you say so. I've brought a good many into this world, Mr. Herrick, but very few have ever made me proud of the fact."

"I fear you're a bit of a pessimist, Doctor."

"No, no, I'm only honest. With myself, that is. In my dealings with others, sir, I'm—just an ordinary New Englander."

"That sounds hard on New Englanders," said Wade with a smile. "Do you mean to say that they're not honest?"

"New Englanders are honest according to their lights, Mr. Herrick, but their lights are sometimes dim. Shall we say this evening for our call on the ladies? Miss Walton has with her a Miss Mullett, a very dear and estimable girl who resides with her in the role of companion. I say girl, but you mustn't be deceived. When you get to sixty-odd you'll find that any lady under fifty is still a girl to you. Miss Mullett, through regrettable circumstances, was overlooked by the seekers after wives and is what you would call a maiden lady. She plays a remarkable hand of cribbage, Mr. Herrick."

"This evening will suit me perfectly, Doctor."

"Then shall we say about half-past seven? We don't keep very late hours in Eden Village. We sup at six, make our calls at seven or half-past, and go to bed promptly at ten. A light in a window after ten o'clock indicates but one thing, illness."

"How about burglars?" laughed Wade.

"Burglars? Bless my soul, we never have 'em, sir. Sometimes a tramp, but never a burglar. Even tramps don't bother us much." The Doctor chuckled as he rescued his hat and cane from beside his chair. "Zenas Prout tells a story to show why Eden Village is exempt. We have a lady here, Mr. Herrick, who should have been of rights a descendant of old Colonel Phelps, Ed's grandfather on his mother's side. The old Colonel's name was synonymous for—let us say self-denial. The lady in question is a very estimable lady, sir, oh, very estimable, but, while she is probably our richest citizen, she is extremely careful and saving. Zenas says a tramp stopped at her door once and asked for food. Miss Cousins —there, I didn't mean to give her name! But no matter—Miss Cousins brought him a slice of stale bread thinly spread with butter. Zenas says the tramp looked from the bread to Miss Cousins, who, I should explain is extremely thin in face and figure, and back to the bread. Then he held it out to her. 'Lady,' he said, 'I haven't the heart to take this from you. You need it more than I do. Eat it yourself!'"

Under cover of Wade's appreciative laughter the Doctor made his adieux, promising to call again at half-past seven. Wade watched him depart down the street, very erect and a trifle pompous, his gold-headed stick serving no other purpose than that of ornament. Then he went indoors and walked to the mirror.

"Gee!" he muttered, "I wish my trunk were here!"

VIII.

The parlor at The Cedars was very different from that in the Craig cottage. It was pretty and comfortable, with lamps that diffused a cheerful, mellow glow over the lower half of the room and left the upper in pleasantly mysterious gloom. There was much old-fashioned furniture —such as the spindle-legged card table at which Miss Mullett and the

Doctor were deeply absorbed in cribbage—but enough comfortable modern chairs had been provided to render martyrdom unnecessary. The four windows were hung with bright creton and muslin, and the dull-green carpet neither stared one out of countenance nor made one fearful to set foot upon it. It was a jolly, chummy sort of carpet that seemed to say, "Walk on me all you want to, and don't be afraid to spill your crumbs; I like crumbs." A very large tortoise-shell cat lay stretched along the arm of the couch, half asleep, and purred as Eve dipped her fingers in the long fur. The windows on the side of the room were open and the draperies swayed gently with the little breeze. Wade, seated at the other end of the couch from his hostess, was feeling happy and inexplicably elated.

"I feel quite guilty about this morning," Eve was saying. "I'm afraid I wasn't very polite. Did I—did I smile?"

"If you didn't, you were a saint," answered Wade. "It's a wonder to me you didn't howl!"

"It was funny, though, wasn't it? Now that it's all over, I mean; now that I've apologized and Carrie has apologized for me and you've apologized. You did look so—so utterly dumfounded!"

"I was!" replied Wade grimly. "For a moment I thought I'd had a sunstroke or something and was out of my head. At first, when I came in and saw you standing there, I thought—it was a foolish thing to think, of course—but I thought you had come to call on me!"

"Again?"

"Again? I'm afraid I don't—"

"Now let's be honest, Mr. Herrick. You did see me the—the first time, didn't you?"

"Just as you wish," laughed Wade. "I did or I didn't."

"You did. I wish you hadn't, but I know you did. I wonder what you thought of me!"

"I—there wasn't much chance to think anything," answered Wade evasively. "You didn't stay long enough."

"I was going by and saw the windows open and couldn't think what to make of it, you see," she explained. "The cottage has been closed up so long that it was quite breath-taking to see it open. My only idea was that it was being aired out. So I thought I'd take a peep. I wanted to see inside, for once I spent a whole day there with Aunt Mary, when I was just a little bit of a girl, and I wondered whether it would look the same. If you think you were surprised this morning when you came in and found me confronting you, what do you suppose I was when I looked in that window and right into your face? Don't you think we're quits now?"

"I reckon we are. Only you didn't make such an ass of yourself as I did. You had presence of mind to get away. In fact you got away so quick I wasn't sure whether I'd seen you or just imagined you. If I hadn't found a lilac bloom on the ground out there I reckon I'd have been sort of worried about myself."

"Did I drop it?"

"You must have. You're fond of it, aren't you?" He nodded at the tiny spray tucked in the front of her white gown.

"Very. And I'm always sorry when it goes. This, I fear, is the very last. It was later this year than usual; last summer it was almost all gone when we got here."

"It's awfully sweet," said Wade. "Driving into the village the other day the fragrance was almost the first thing that struck me. I reckon when I go back West my memory of Eden Village will be perfumed with lilac.

"That's very pretty," said Eve. "Coup-ling lilacs with the West reminds me of something that happened once when I was out there with papa."

Wade's glance wavered and shifted to the couple at the card table. She knew, after all, or suspected!

"It was quite a few years ago. Papa was interested in some mines in Nevada, and he took me out with him one spring on a business trip. Coming back we stopped one morning at a little town. I don't remember whether it was in Nevada or Colorado, and I've forgotten the funny, outlandish name it had. There were just a few houses and stores there. Papa and I got out of the Pullman and walked up and down the station platform. Just across the road was a little frame house and in front of it was a lilac bush just full of blooms. It seemed so strange to find such a thing out there, and the blossoms were so lovely that I called papa's attention to it. 'I do wish I could have some!' I said. There were some men standing about the station, great big rough-looking men, miners or ranchers, I suppose. One of them heard me and whipped off his hat. 'Do the flowers please you, ma'am?' he asked. He looked so kind of wild and ferocious that I was too startled to answer him at first, 'Cause if they do,' he went on, 'I'll get all you want.' 'Indeed they do,' I said, 'but they're not yours, are they?' 'No, ma'am, they're yourn,' he said. He pulled out a big knife, strode across to the bush and began cutting the poor thing all to pieces. 'Oh, please don't!' I cried. 'That's more than enough!' 'Just as you say, ma'am,' and he came back with a dozen great branches of them. I took them and thanked him. I told him it was dear of him to give them to me and I did hope he hadn't spoiled his bush. He—he—well, he emptied his mouth of a great deal of tobacco juice, wiped his big hand across it and said: 'It ain't my bush, ma'am, but you're just as welcome to them lilocks as if it was. There ain't nothin' in this town a pretty girl can't have for the askin'!' Thank goodness, the conductor cried 'All aboard' just then and I ran up the steps. There wasn't any reply I could have made to that, was there? As the train went off we could see the other men on the platform laughing and hitting my friend on the back, and enjoying it all greatly. But wasn't it dear of him?"

"Yes," answered Wade, warmly. "They're like that out there, though rough and uncultured, maybe, but kind and big-hearted underneath. I dare say that incident made him feel so good that he went out and shot a Greaser."

"Oh, I hope not!" laughed Eve. "But he looked as though he might have shot dozens of them, one every morning for breakfast! The flowers lasted me all the way to Chicago. The porter put them in the ice-water tank and I picked fresh lilacs every day."

Wade wondered whether she had forgotten another incident, which must have happened on the evening of that same day. He hoped she had, and then he hoped she hadn't. If she recalled it she made no mention of it, nor did the smiling unconsciousness of her face suggest that she connected him with her trip in the remotest degree. He felt a little bit aggrieved. It wasn't flattering to be forgotten so completely.

"You said your father was interested in some mines in Nevada. Do you mind telling me the name?"

"The New Century Consolidated, they were called."

"Oh, that was too bad," exclaimed Wade, regretfully. "That property never was any good. The whole thing was a swindle from first to last. Was your father very badly hit?"

"Ruined," answered Eve, simply. "He had to sell everything he had. They had made him a director, you see, and when the exposure came he paid up his share. The lawyer said he didn't have to, but he insisted. He was right, don't you think, Mr. Herrick?"

"No—well, perhaps. I don't know. It depends how you look at it, I reckon."

"There was only one way to look at it, wasn't there? Either it was right or it was wrong. Father believed it was right."

"So it was! But plenty of men would have hidden behind the law. I wish your father might have bought into our property instead of the New Century. I wanted Ed to write to him; we needed money badly at first, and I'd heard Ed speak of him once; but he wouldn't do it; said his uncle wouldn't have anything to do with any schemes of his."

"I'm afraid he was right," said Eve, sadly. "When I was a little girl my father and Ed's father had some sort of a misunderstanding and would never have anything to do with each other afterwards. It made it very hard for mamma, for she and Aunt Mary were very fond of each other. Please tell me about Cousin Edward, Mr. Herrick. I think I only saw him once or twice in my life, but he was my cousin just the same, and now that he's dead I suddenly realize that all the time I was unconsciously taking a sort of comfort out of the knowledge that somewhere I had some one that belonged to me, even if I never saw him and hardly knew him. What was he like?"

"A big, silent, good-hearted fellow. I think there was a resemblance to you, Miss Walton. He was dark complexioned, with almost black eyes, but—there's something in your expression at times—that reminds me of Ed." Wade frowned and studied the girl's face. "But I have a photograph of him at the Camp. I'll send for it. Shall I?"

"It wouldn't be too much trouble?"

"No trouble at all. I'll just send a wire to Whitehead, the superintendent. I met Ed in a queer way. It was at Cripple Creek. I'd been there almost a year. After my mother died there wasn't anything to keep me at home in Virginia, and there wasn't much money. So I hiked out to Colorado, thinking about all I'd have to do was to cinch up my belt and start to pick up gold nuggets in the streets. The best I could find was work with a shovel in one of the mines over Victor way. Then I got work in another mine handling explosives. I got in front of a missed hole one fine day and was blown down a slope with about a hundred tons of rock on top of me. As luck had it, however, the big ones wedged over me and I wasn't hurt much, just scratched up a bit."

"But that was wonderful!" breathed Eve.

"Yes, it was sort of funny. I was covered up from one in the afternoon until five, quite conscious all the time and pretty well scared. You see, I couldn't help wondering just what would happen if the rocks should settle. My eyes got the worst of it and I had to stay in the hospital about a month. But I'm afraid I'm boring you. I was just leading up to my meeting with Ed."

"Boring me! Don't be absurd! Then what happened?"

"Well, after I got out of the hospital I bought a burro and a tent and hiked out for the Sangre—for the southern part of the State. I still had some money coming to me for work when the trouble happened, and after I got out I cashed an accident policy I'd luckily taken out a month before. I stayed in the mountains pretty much all summer prospecting. I found the biggest bunch of rock I'd ever seen, but no yellow iron—I mean gold. Came sort of near starving before I got out. I sold my outfit and went back to Cripple and struck another job with the shovel and pick, digging prospect ditches. It was pretty tiresome work and pretty cold, too. So when I'd got a month's wages I told the boss he'd either have to put me underground or I'd quit. I said I was a miner and not a Dago. You see, I felt independently rich with a month's wages in my jeans—pockets, that is. The boss said I could quit. I've been wondering ever since," laughed Wade, "whether I quit or was fired."

"That was lovely," said Eve. "Oh, dear, I've often wished I'd been a man!"

"H'm; well, every one to his taste. But look here, Miss Walton, you're certain I'm not boring you to death?"

"Quite. What did you do with all that money? And how much did a month's wages amount to?"

"About ninety dollars. You get three a day and work seven days a week. But, of course, I owed a good deal of that ninety by the time I got it. Well, I paid my bills and then did a fool thing. I got my laundry out of the Chinaman's, put on a stiff shirt and went over to Colorado Springs. It just seemed that I had to have a glimpse of—well, you know; respectability—dress clothes—music—flowers. I remember how stiff and uncomfortable that shirt felt and how my collar scratched my neck. When I got over to the Springs I ran across some folks I'd known back home in Virginia. Richmond folks, they were. I dined with them and had a fine time. I forgot to tell them I'd been pushing a shovel with the Pinheads—that is, Swedes. They asked me to be sure and visit them when I went back to Virginia for Christmas, for of course I would go! I told 'em I'd do that very thing. Rather a joke, wasn't it? If railroads had been selling at forty dollars a pair I couldn't have bought a headlight! I went back to Cripple the next day, having spent most of my money, feeling sort of grouchy and down on my luck. That night I thought I'd have a go at the wheel—roulette, you know. I'd steered pretty clear of that sort of thing up to then, but I didn't much care that night what happened. I only had about fifteen dollars and I played it dollar by dollar and couldn't win once. Finally I was down to my last. I remember I took that out of my pocket and looked at it quite awhile. Then I put it back and started to go. But before I'd reached the door I concluded that a dollar wasn't much better than none in Cripple, and so I went back to the table. It was pretty crowded and I had to work my way in until I could reach it. Just when I got my dollar out again and was going to toss it on, blind, some one took hold of my arm and pulled me around. I'd never seen the fellow before and I started to get peeved. But he—may I use his words? They weren't polite, but they were persuasive. Said he: 'Put that back in your pocket, you damned fool, and come out of here."

Wade looked anxiously at his audience to see if she was shocked. She didn't look so; only eager and sympathetic. He went on.

"Well, I went. He lugged me over to his room across the street and—and was hospitable. He made me talk and I told him how I was fixed. He told me who he was and said he thought he could find a job for me. And he did. He was partner with a man named Hogan in an assay office and knew a good many mine managers and superintendents. The next day I went to work running an air-drill at four dollars a day. That's how I met Ed. We got to be pretty good friends after that. Later I went over and roomed with him. He was only two years older than I, but he always seemed about ten. I told him about the Sangre—about the country I'd prospected in the summer and we agreed to go over it together. In the spring, when the snow was off, we started out. We bought a good outfit, two burros, a good tent, and everything we could need. We expected to be away all summer, but we struck gold about five weeks after we reached the mountains. Struck it rich, too. All that summer we slaved like Dagoes and by fall we had a prospect good enough to show any one. But we needed money for development, and it was then I suggested to Ed that he write to Mr. Walton. You see, I'd heard a good deal about his folks and about Eden Village by that time. Evenings, after you've had supper and while you're smoking your pipe, there isn't much to talk about except your people and things back in God's country. And we'd told each other about everything we knew by autumn. But Ed wouldn't consider his uncle; said we'd have to find some one else to put in the money. So we had a clean-up and I started East with a trunk full of samples and a pocket full of papers. Ed gave me the names of some men to see. As luck had it, I didn't have to go further than Omaha. The first man I tackled bit and three months later we started development. Ed and I kept a controlling interest. Now the—" Wade pulled himself up, gulped and hesitated—"the mine is the richest in that district and is getting better all the time."

"It's like a fairy tale, almost," said Eve.

"What is the name of the mine, Mr. Herrick?"

"Well—er—we usually just called it 'The Mine.' It isn't listed on the exchange, you see. There aren't any shares on the market."

"Really? But I wasn't thinking of investing, Mr. Herrick," responded Eve, dryly. "If there's any reason why I shouldn't know the name, that's sufficient."

Wade observed her troubledly.

"I—I beg your pardon, Miss Walton. I didn't mean to be rude. The mine has a name, of course, and—and sometime I'll tell it to you. But just now —there's a reason—"

"It sounds," laughed Eve, "as though you were talking of a cereal coffee. Indeed, though, I don't want to know if you don't want me to."

"But I do! That is—sometime—"

"I understand; it's a guilty secret. But you were telling me about my cousin. When did he die, Mr. Herrick?"

"Last August. We'd both been working pretty hard and Ed was sort of run down, I reckon. He got typhoid and went quick. I got him to Pueblo as soon as I learned what the trouble was, but the doctor there said he never had a chance. We buried him in Pueblo."

Wade was looking down at his roughened hands and spoke so low that Eve had to bend forward a little to hear him.

"It—it was a pretty decent funeral," he added simply. "There were seven carriages."

"Really?" she murmured.

"Yes." He raised his head and looked at her a trifle wistfully. "You can't understand just what Ed's death meant to me, Miss Walton. You see, he was about the only real friend I ever had, the only fellow I ever got real close to. And he was such a thoroughbred, and—and was so darn—so mighty good to me! I tell you, it sort of knocked me out for awhile."

"I'm sorry I didn't know him," said Eve, softly. "I'm sure I'd have liked him as well as you did. And perhaps he'd have liked me."

"I'm sure of that," said Wade with conviction.

"I suppose he never spoke of me?"

"Only once, I think. Before he died he told me he had made a will and left me his share of the mine and everything else he had. I—oh, well, I didn't like it and said so. 'You'll have to take it,' he answered. 'There's no one else to leave it to; I've got no relatives left except an uncle and a cousin, and they have all the money they need. You see, he didn't know about—'"

"I understand. And even had papa been alive he would have accepted nothing from Edward, I'm certain."

"But you—"

"Nor I."

"I'm sorry to hear you say that," said Wade, frowningly. "I've been thinking that perhaps—something might be done. There's so much money, Miss Walton, and it doesn't belong to me. Don't you think—"

"No." Eve shook her head gently, but decisively. "It's nice of you to want it, Mr. Herrick, but you mustn't think any more about it. Papa would never have allowed me to accept any of Cousin Edward's property if he had been alive, and I shan't do it now that he is dead. We won't speak about that any more, please. Tell me how you came to visit Eden Village. To see the house you'd inherited?"

"Yes. Ed wanted me to. He was very fond of this place and fond of the house. 'I'd rather you always kept it,' he told me. 'If the time ever comes when you have to sell it, all right; but until then see that it's looked after and kept up.' So this summer, when I found I was going to have a vacation—the first real one for six years, Miss Walton—I decided that the first thing I'd do would be to come here and look after Ed's place."

"Then yours is only a flying visit? I'm sorry."

"No, I think I shall stay some time," replied Wade. "I like it immensely. It's so different from where I've been. And, besides, the house needs looking after. I think I'll have it painted."

"Then you'll be sure to make mistakes," laughed Eve. "Or perhaps you'll paint it a different color from this?"

"No, I shan't; white it must be. Then, you see, I'll have every excuse for mistaking this house for my own."

"I hope you won't feel that you need an excuse to come here, Mr. Herrick. We're not a ceremonious people here. We can't afford to be; neighbors are too scarce."

Wade thanked her and there was a moment's silence. Then Eve, who had been smilingly watching the players, turned with lowered voice.

"And sometimes when you come to see us, Mr. Herrick, won't you come through the gate in the hedge, please?"

"Certainly," he answered, looking a little puzzled.

"Does that sound queer?" she asked with a soft laugh. "I suppose it does. There was a time when the dwellers in your house and in mine used that gate in the hedge as my poor old grandfather meant they should. Perhaps I have a fancy to see it used so again. Or perhaps that isn't the reason at all. You have your secret; we'll call this mine. Maybe some day we'll tell our secrets."

"Is that a promise?" he asked, eagerly.

She hesitated a moment. Then, "If you like," she answered, smiling across at him.

"Good! Then let us have it all shipshape, in contract form."

"Oh, you business men!"

"I hereby agree to tell you before I leave Eden Village the name of my mine, and you agree to tell me why—why—"

"Why you are to come to see us by way of the gate in the hedge. Agreed, signed, sealed, and delivered in the presence of Miss Caroline Mullett and Doctor Joseph Crimmins."

"Eh?" asked the Doctor. "What's that? I heard my name spoken, didn't I?"

"You did, Doctor, but quite respectfully," answered Eve.

"Respectfully!" grumbled the Doctor. "That's all age gets, just respect! Thirty years ago, madam, you wouldn't have dared to respect me! I beg your pardon, Miss Mullett; you are right, it is my first count. Fifteen-two, fifteen-four, fifteen-six, and a pair's eight and one's nine. And that puts me out!"

"Brute!" said Miss Mullett.

"Who won?" asked Eve.

"I, Miss Eve, but an empty victory since I have incurred this dear lady's displeasure," replied the Doctor, arising. "I had the misfortune to run out when she needed but one to win, an unpardonable crime in the game of cribbage, Mr. Herrick."

"I'm not sure we wouldn't hang you for that out our way, Doctor," said Wade, with a smile.

"Well, something ought to be done to him," grumbled Miss Mullett, closing the cribbage box with a snap.

"Madam, leave me to the reproaches of my conscience," advised the offender.

"Your conscience!" jeered Miss Mullett. "You haven't any. You're a doctor."

"Mr. Herrick, let us be going, I pray.

"'From pole to pole the thunder roars aloud, And broken lightnings flash from ev'ry cloud.'

"Besides which, sir, it is close upon ten o'clock, I see, the bed-hour of our virtuous village. Miss Mullett, I shall pray for your forgiveness. Miss Eve, I trust you to say a good word for me. If the storm clears, do you hang a white handkerchief from the window there and I, going by, will see it and be comforted." The Doctor laid a hand on Wade's shoulder and, with a mischievous glance at Miss Mullett, whispered hoarsely: "Stern in her anger, Mr. Herrick, but of an amiable and forgiving disposition."

"I'll forgive you when I've had my revenge," answered Miss Mullett, laughingly.

"Ah, the clouds break! Let us be gone, Mr. Herrick, while the sun shines on our pathway!"

When the front door had closed Miss Mullett turned eagerly to Eve.

"Sit down, dear, and tell me! Was he nice? What did he say?"

IX.

"'When He cometh, when He cometh
To make up His jewels,
All His jewels, precious jewels,
His loved and His own.
Like the stars of the morning,
His bright crown adorning,
They shall shine—'"

"Mr. Herring, sir, breakfast's most ready."

"So am I," answered Wade, throwing open the door. "It certainly smells good, Zephania. Got lots of coffee?"

"Oh, yes, Mr. Herring."

"Herrick, Zephania."

"Yes, sir; excuse me; Herrick."

After breakfast Zene, as his father and Zephania called him, or Zenas Third, as he was known to the Village, appeared with Wade's trunk on a wheelbarrow. Zenas Third was a big, broad-shouldered youth of twenty with a round, freckled, smiling face and eager yellow-brown eyes. He always reminded Wade of an amiable animated pumpkin. Wade got his fishing tackle out of the trunk and he and Zenas Third started off for a day's fishing.

They took the road past The Cedars, Wade viewing the house on the chance of seeing the ladies. But although he failed and was a little disappointed he did not escape observation himself.

"There goes Mr. Herrick with Zenas Third," announced Miss Mullett, hurrying cautiously to the sitting-room window. As she had been in the act of readjusting her embroidery hoops when she arose, her efforts to secure all the articles in her lap failed and the hoops went circling off in different directions. "They're going fishing, Eve."

"Are they?" asked Eve from the old mahogany desk by the side window, with only a glance from her writing.

"Yes, and—*Did* you see where those hoops rolled to?"

"No, I didn't notice. But your handkerchief is over by the couch and you're stepping on a skein of linen."

"So I am." Miss Mullett rescued and reassembled her things and sat down again. "Are you very busy, dear?"

"No." Eve sighed impatiently and laid her pen down. "I'm not at all busy. I wish I were. I can't seem to write this morning."

"I'm so glad. Not that you can't write, of course, but that you're not busy. I want to talk."

"Talk on." Eve placed her hands behind her head and eyed the few lines of writing distastefully.

"But I want you to talk, too," said Miss Mullett, snipping a thread with her tiny scissors.

"I haven't anything to say."

"Nonsense, dear! There's always plenty to say. Why, I'm sure if I lived to be a thousand, I'd not be talked out. There's always so many interesting things to talk about."

"And what is it this morning?" asked Eve, smiling across at the sleek head bent above the embroidery frame.

"Mr. Herrick. Tell me what you think of him, Eve."

"I haven't thought—much."

"But you ought to. I'm positive he is very much impressed, dear."

"Really? With what?"

"With you." Eve laughed, softly.

"Carrie, you're incorrigible! You won't be satisfied until you've got me married to some one."

"Of course I shan't. I don't intend that you shall make the mistake I did."

"You didn't make a mistake, you dear thing. Your mistake would have been to marry. You'd never have been contented with just one man, Carrie; you know you think every one you meet is perfectly beautiful.'"

"Because I haven't one of my very own," replied Miss Mullett, tranquilly. "I made a great mistake in not marrying. I would have been happier married, I'm sure. Every woman ought to have a man to look after; it keeps her from worrying over trifles."

"Do you think I worry over trifles?" asked Eve.

"You're worrying over that story this minute."

"If I am, it's unkind of you to call my stories trifles. Please remember that if it wasn't for the stories, such as they are, I couldn't afford marmalade with my tea."

"And you probably couldn't afford me," said Miss Mullett, "and I guess I'm a good deal like marmalade myself—half sweet and half bitter." Miss Mullett laughed at the conceit.

"Anyway, dear, you don't cloy," said Eve. "But you're not like marmalade the least bit; you're—you're like a nice currant jelly, just tart enough to be pleasant. How's that?"

"Just so long as you don't call me a pickle I don't mind," replied the other. Presently: "You must acknowledge that he's very attractive, dear."

"Who?" asked Eve, coming suddenly out of her thoughts.

"Mr. Herrick. And I think he has the most wonderful voice, too; don't you? It's so deep and—and manly."

"Carrie, if his Satanic Majesty called on us, you'd be telling me after he'd gone how manly he looked!"

"Well, I'm not one to deny the resemblance between man and the Devil," responded Miss Mullett, with a chuckle. "I dare say that's why we like them so—the men, I mean."

"Does Mr. Herrick strike you as being somewhat devilish?" inquired Eve, idly.

"N-no, I suppose not. Not too much so, at least. I think he must be very kind; he has such nice eyes. He's the sort of man that makes a lovely husband."

Eve clapped her hands to her ears, laughing.

"Carrie, stop it! I refuse to listen to any more laudations of Mr. Herrick! Think how the poor man's ears must burn!"

"Let them. He has very nice ears, Eve. Did you notice how small and close they were?"

"I did not!" declared Eve despairingly. "Nor did I specially observe his teeth or his hair or his feet, or—"

"But you noticed the scar on his face, didn't you?"

"Yes, I couldn't very well help doing that," owned Eve. "Any more than I could help noticing his hands."

"So strong looking, aren't they?" asked Miss Mullett, eagerly.

"Are they? I thought them rather ugly."

"Oh, how can you say so? Just think of all the wonderful things those hands must have done! And as for the scar, I thought it gave him quite a distinguished air, didn't you?"

"Carrie Mullett, I am not interested in Mr. Herrick. If you say another word about him before luncheon—"

"You can say that if you like," interrupted Miss Mullett placidly, "but you are interested in him, my dear."

"Carrie!"

"Then why can't you write your story? Oh, you can't fool me, my dear!"

Eve turned a disdainful back and picked up her pen, resentful of the warmth that she felt creeping into her cheeks.

Miss Mullett smiled and drew a new thread from the skein.

X.

"You observe," said Wade the next morning, "I come through the gate in the hedge."

The intermittent showers of yesterday afternoon and night had cleaned the June world, and the four ancient cedars from which the Walton place had received its name, and in the broken shade of which Eve was reading, exhaled a spicy odor under the influence of moisture and warmth. Eve, a slim white figure against the dark-green of the foliage, the sun flecking her waving hair, looked up, smiled and laid her book down.

"Good morning," she said. "Have you come to help me be lazy?"

"If you need help," he replied. "I brought these. They're not much, but I think they're the last in the village." He handed her a half-dozen sprays of purple lilac, small and in some places already touched with brown.

"Oh," she said, "they're lovely!" She buried her face in them and crooned over them delightedly. Witnessing her pleasure, Wade had no regrets for his hour's search over the length and breadth of Eden Village. She laid them in her lap and looked up curiously. "Where did you get them? Not from your hedge?"

"Oh, I just stopped at the florist's as I came along," he laughed. "He apologized for them and wanted me to take orchids, but I told him they were for the Lilac Girl."

"Is that me?" smiled Eve. "Thank you very much." She made a little bow. "I feel dreadfully impolite and inhospitable, Mr. Herrick, at not asking you to sit down, but—you see!" She waved a hand before her.

"There's nothing but the ground, and that's damp, I'm afraid. So let us go indoors. Besides, I must put these in water."

"Please don't," he begged. "The ground isn't damp where the sun shines, and I wouldn't mind if it were. If I'm not keeping you from your book I'll sit down here. May I?"

"You'll catch rheumatism or ague or something else dreadful," she warned.

"Not I," he laughed. "I've never been sick a day in my life, unless it was after I'd got mixed up with dynamite that time. Don't you think you might wear those lilacs?"

"Surely not all of them. One, perhaps." She tucked a spray in at the bosom of her white waist. "You haven't told me yet where you got them. Have you been stealing?"

"Some I stole, some I begged, and some I—just took. I think I can truthfully declare, though, that there is not another bit of lilac at this moment in the whole village. I went on a foraging expedition after breakfast and there is the result. I've examined every bush and hedge with a microscope."

"And all that trouble for me!" she exclaimed. "I'm sure I'm flattered." A little flush of rose-pink crept into her clear cheeks. "Do you know, Mr. Herrick, you're a perfectly delightful neighbor? Last night fish, to-day flowers! And I haven't thanked you for the fish, have I? They were delicious, and it was good of you to send them. Especially as Zenas Third said you didn't have very good luck."

"No, we didn't catch many," answered Wade, "but we had a good time. I was sorry I couldn't send more, though."

"More! Pray how many trout do you think two ladies of delicate appetites can eat, Mr. Herrick? You sent six, and we didn't begin to eat all of those."

"Really? They were little chaps, too. I'm glad you liked them. Next time I hope I'll have some better ones to offer. Zenas and I are going to try again the first cloudy day."

"I hope you have good luck." There was a moment's silence. Eve raised the lilacs to her face again and over the tips of the sprays shot a glance at Wade. He had crossed his legs under him and was feeling for his pipe. He looked up and their eyes met.

"I'm afraid I can't offer you any tobacco," she said.

"I've got plenty," he laughed, "if you don't mind my smoking."

"Not a bit. Perhaps I should call Carrie. I think she likes the smell of tobacco better than any perfume she knows."

"Is she well?" asked Wade, contritely. "I should have asked before, but—you—something put it out of my head."

"Quite well, thanks. She's making something for luncheon and has forbidden me the kitchen. It's a surprise. Do you like surprises, Mr. Herrick?"

"Some. It depends on the nature of them."

"I suppose it does. An earthquake, for instance, would be a rather disagreeable surprise, wouldn't it?"

"Decidedly. I can imagine a surprise that would be distinctly pleasant, though," said Wade, giving a great deal of attention to the selection of a match from his silver case. "For instance, if you were to give me a small piece of that lilac for my buttonhole."

"That would surprise you?" laughed Eve. "Then I'm to understand that you think me ungenerous?"

"No, indeed, I was—was considering my unworthiness."

"Such humility is charming," answered Eve, breaking off a tiny spray and tossing it to him. "There; aren't you awfully surprised? Please look so."

Wade struck an attitude and made a grimace which to a third person would have indicated wild alarm.

"Oh, dear," laughed Eve, "if that's your idea of looking pleasant I'd hate to see you in an earthquake!"

Wade placed the spray in his buttonhole. "Thank you," he said, "I shall have quite a collection—"

"You were going to say?" asked Eve politely as he paused.

"I was going to say"—he paused again. "You know I already have a spray of this that belongs to you." He shot a quick, curious glance at her.

"You have? And where did you get it?"

Wade lighted his pipe very deliberately.

"You dropped it outside my window the other day."

"Oh!" said Eve, with a careless laugh.

"I'm afraid that must be withered by this time."

"It is," said Wade. There was no reply to this, and he looked up to find her gazing idly at the pages of her book, which she was ruffling with her fingers. "I'm keeping you from reading," he said.

"No, I don't want to read. It's not interesting."

"May I see what it is?" She held the cover up for his inspection.

"Have you read it?" she asked. He shook his head slowly.

"I don't read many novels, and those I do read I forget all about the next minute. Of course I try to keep up with the important ones, the ones folks always ask you about, like Mrs. Humphrey Ward's and Miss Wharton's."

"Yes? And do you like them?"

"I suppose so," he replied, dubiously. "I think the last one I read was 'The Fruit of Mirth.' I didn't care very much for that, did you? If I'd had my way I'd have passed around the morphine to the whole bunch early in the book."

Eve smiled. "I'm afraid you wouldn't care for this one either," she said, indicating the book in her lap. "I heard this described as 'forty chapters of agony and two words of relief.'"

"'The End,' eh? That was clever. You write stories yourself, don't you?"

"Of a sort, stories for little children about fairies, usually. They don't amount to much."

"I'll bet they're darn—mighty good," said Wade, stoutly.

"I wish they were 'darned good,'" she laughed. "If they were they'd sell better. I used to write little things for our college paper, and then, when papa died, and there wasn't very much left after the executors had got through, writing seemed about the only thing I could do. I took some stories to the magazine that papa was editor of, and they were splendid to me. They couldn't use them, but they told me where to take them and I sold several. That was the beginning. Now I'm fast becoming a specialist in 'Once-Upon-a-Time' stories."

"I'd like to read some of them," said Wade. "I'm awfully fond of fairy stories." "Oh, but these are very young fairy stories, like—like this one." Eve pulled a pencilled sheet of paper from the pages of her book, smiled, hesitated, and read: "'Once upon a time there was a Fairy Princess whose name was Dewdrop. She lived in a beautiful Blue Palace deep in the heart of a Canterbury Bell that swayed to and fro, to and fro, at the top of the garden wall. And when the sun shone against the walls of her palace it was filled with a lovely lavender light, and when the moon shone it was all asparkle with silver. It was quite the most desirable palace in the whole garden, for it was the only one that had a view over the great high wall, and many fairies envied her because she lived in it. One of those who wanted the Blue Palace for himself was a very wicked fairy who lived under a toadstool nearby. He was so terribly wicked that I don't like to even tell you about him. He never got up to breakfast when he was called, he never did as he was told, and he used to sit for hours on top of his toadstool, putting out his tongue at all the other fairies who flew by. And he did lots and lots of other things, too, that only a thoroughly depraved fairy could ever think of, like putting cockleburs in the nests where the baby birds lived, and making them very uncomfortable, and chasing the moles about underground, and making a squeaking noise like a hungry weasel, and scaring the poor little moles almost to death. Oh, I could tell you lots of dreadful things about the wicked fairy if I wanted to. His name was Nettlesting, and his father and mother were both dead, and he lived all alone with his grandmother, who simply spoiled him! And—'and that's all there is. How do you like it?"

"Bully," said Wade. "What's the rest of it?"

"I don't know. That's as far as I've got. I suppose, though, that the wicked fairy tried to oust the Princess from the Blue Palace, and there were perfectly scandalous doings in Fairyland."

"I hope you'll finish it," said Wade. "I rather like Nettlesting."

"Oh, but you mustn't! The moral is that fairies who don't get up to breakfast when they're called always come to some bad end. You must like the Princess and think the wicked fairy quite detestable."

"Can't help it," Wade replied, apologetically. "The wicked fairy had a sense of humor and I like him. That chasing the moles around and squeaking like a weasel appeals to me. I'll bet that's just what I'd do if I were a fairy!"

"I know," said Eve, nodding her head sympathetically. "I'm ashamed to say it, but I always like the wicked fairies, too. It's dreadfully hard sometimes for me to give them their deserts. I'm afraid I don't make them mean enough. What is your idea of a thoroughly depraved fairy, Mr. Herrick?"

Wade frowned a moment, thinking deeply.

"Well," he said finally, "you might have him go around and upset the bird-nests and spill the little birds out. How would that do?"

"Beautifully! Oh, he *would* be wicked; even I couldn't like a fairy who did that. Thank you ever so much, Mr. Herrick; I would never have thought of that myself. What a beautifully wicked imagination you must have! I'll make Nettlesting do that very thing."

"No, don't change him, please; I like him the way he is. When will that story be published?"

"Oh, I may never finish it, and, if I do, it may never be accepted."

Wade pondered a minute. Then—"Of course, you know it's perfect nonsense," he charged.

"My story? Isn't that a little cruel, Mr. Herrick?"

"I don't mean your story. I mean the idea of you having to write things to make a living when—when there's all that money that really belongs to you. I wish, Miss Walton, you'd look at it sensibly."

"Mr. Herrick, you're not flattering any more."

"Can't help it," answered Wade, doggedly. "You ought to consider the matter from—from a practical point of view. Now you can't deny—"

"A woman can deny anything," laughed Eve, "especially if it's logic."

"This isn't logic; it's incontrovertible fact."

"Good gracious! No, I don't believe I'd have the courage to deny such a thing as that. I'm sure it would be quite unlawful, wouldn't it, Mr. Herrick?"

"Won't you please be serious?" he begged.

"No, not to-day, thank you."

"Then we'll talk about it some other day."

"No, but we won't, please. I'd like you to understand, Mr. Herrick, that I appreciate your—your kindness, your generosity, but all the argument in the world won't shake my resolution to take none of Cousin Edward's money. Now we understand each other, don't we?"

"I suppose so," answered Wade, regretfully. "But you're making a mistake, Miss Walton. Won't you just think about it?' Won't you take advice from—from your friends?"

"The last thing I'd do," Eve replied, smilingly. "One's friends are the very ones to avoid when you want unbiased advice. For instance, there's Carrie Mullett. I told her what you said the other night, and what do you suppose her advice was?"

"I'm sure it was sensible," said Wade. "She's a very sensible, as well as a very charming, lady."

"H'm; well, she said: 'Accept enough to live on, my dear. Your father would never have wanted you to be dependent on yourself for your living.'"

"Well?" asked Wade, hopefully.

"She never knew papa," replied Eve. "Besides, I am not dependent on myself for my living. I have enough to live on even if I never sold a thing. I'm not so poverty-stricken as you imagine."

"If you'd talk it over with a lawyer—"

"But it isn't a question of law, Mr. Herrick. It's something between me and my conscience, you see. And surely," she ended with a smile, "you wouldn't consult a lawyer about an affair of conscience? Why, I might have to explain what a conscience was!"

"Well," said Wade, grimly. "I've made no promises, and I haven't given up yet. And you'll find, Miss Walton, that I'm a tiresome chap when it comes to having my own way."

"And you'll find, Mr. Herrick, that I'm a stubborn woman when it comes to having mine. There, the battle is on!"

"And I shall win," said Wade, looking up at her with a sudden gleam in his eyes. For an instant she met his gaze and found herself a little dismayed at some expression she found there. But—

"We'll see," she answered, calmly. "Is it to be war to the knife, Mr. Herrick?"

"I hope it won't come to that," he answered. "But there's another thing I want you to do, and as it's something you can do without wounding your conscience, I hope you will."

"It sounds formidable. What is it, please?"

"Come over this afternoon and have tea, you and Miss Mullett. Will you?"

"Gladly. I haven't had afternoon tea since I left New York."

"Then shall we say four o'clock? Don't fail me, please, Miss Walton, for Zephania and I will be terribly disappointed if you do. It's our first tea, you know."

"Indeed we won't fail you!" answered Eve. "And, please, I like lemon with mine."

All was ready for the guests long before the time appointed, and Wade, attired in his best blue serge, whitest vest, and bluest silk tie, and clean-shaven to a painful degree, paced impatiently between the kitchen, fragrant with the odor of newly-baked cake, and the parlor, less chill and formal than usual under the humanizing influence of several bowls and vases of flowers.

The ladies were quite on time, Miss Mullett looking sweet and cheerful in pink and white, and Eve absolutely lovely and adorable in pale-blue linen that matched her eyes to the fraction of a tone. They settled themselves in the cool parlor and talked while the shades rustled and whispered in the little scented breeze that stole through the open windows. Zephania, starched and ribboned, bore proudly in the best silver tea service, Wade watching the progress of the heavily laden tray across the room with grave anxiety.

"I'd like you to know," he announced when it was safely deposited on the little table at Eve's side, "that this is Zephania's spread. She made the cake herself—and the bread too."

"The dear child!" said Miss Mullett.

"Why, Zephania!" exclaimed Eve.

And Zephania, very proud and rosy, and trying hard to look unconcerned, made her escape just as Doctor Crimmins, happening by, heard the voices and demanded admittance with the head of his cane on the window-sill. That was a very jolly tea-party. The Doctor ate six pieces of cake and drank three cups of tea, praising each impartially between mouthfuls. Wade, eating and drinking spasmodically, told of his adventures in search of lemons.

"Prout's emporium was quite out of them," he explained. "Prout said he had had some a few weeks ago, but they were sold. So I walked over to The Centre and got them there."

Miss Mullett eluded him anxiously and insisted that the Doctor should examine his pulse.

"You ought never to have taken such a walk on such a hot day, Mr. Herrick. The idea! Why, you might have died! Why don't you scold him, Eve?"

Eve's eyebrows went up.

"Why should I scold him, Carrie? Mr. Herrick knew that I liked lemon in my tea and, being a very gallant gentleman, he obtained lemon. You all know that I am quite heartless where my wants are concerned."

"Well, I think it was extremely wrong, Mr. Herrick, and I shan't touch another slice of lemon."

"Which," laughed Eve, "considering that you already have four pieces floating about in your cup, is truly heroic!"

After the ladies had gone the Doctor lingered, and presently, in some strange way, he found himself in the dining-room with the doors carefully closed, saying "Ha! H'm!" and wiping his lips gratefully. He made Wade promise to come and see him, quoted a couplet anent hospitality—neglecting to give the author's name—and took his departure. After supper Wade lighted his pipe and started in the direction of the Doctor's house, but he never got there that evening. For an hour or more he wandered along the quiet, almost deserted street, and smoked and thought and watched the effect of the moonlight amidst the high branches of the elms, finally finding himself back at his own gate, tapping his pipe against the post and watching the red sparks drop.

"It isn't going to be very hard, after all," he murmured.

XI.

June mellowed into July and July moved by in a procession of hot, languorous days and still, warm nights. Sometimes it rained, and then the leaves and flowers, adroop under the sun's ardor, quivered and swayed with delight and scented the moist air with the sweet, faint fragrance of their gratitude. Often the showers came at night, and Wade, lying in bed with doors and windows open, could hear it pattering upon the leaves and drumming musically upon the shingles. And he fancied, too, that he could hear the thankful earth drinking it in with its millions of little thirsty mouths. After such a night he awoke to find the room filled with dewy, perfumed freshness and radiant with sunshine, while out of doors amidst the sparkling leaves the birds trilled pæans to the kindly heavens.

By the middle of July Wade had settled down comfortably into the quiet life of Eden Village. Quiet it was, but far from hum-drum. On the still, mirrored surface of a pool even the dip of an insect's wing will cause commotion. So it was in Eden Village. On the placid surface of existence there the faintest zephyr became a gale that raised waves of excitement; the tiniest happening was an event. It is all a matter of proportion. Wade experienced as much agitation when a corner of the woodshed caught on fire, and he put it out with a broom, as when with forty men behind him, he had fought for hours to save the buildings at the mine two years before. Something of interest was always happening. There was the day when the serpent appeared in Eden. Appropriately enough, it was Eve who discovered it, curled up in the sun right by the gate. Her appeals for assistance brought Wade in a hurry, and the serpent, after an exciting chase through the hedges and flower beds, was finally dispatched. It proved to be an adder of blameless character, but neither Eve nor Miss Mullett had any regrets. Eve declared that a snake was a snake, no matter what any one—meaning Wade—said, and Wade was forced to acknowledge the fact. Armed with a shovel, they marched to the back garden, Wade holding the snake by its unquiet tail, and interred it there, so that Alexander the Great, the tortoise-shell cat, wouldn't eat it and be poisoned. Subsequently the affair had to be discussed in all its aspects by Eve and Wade in the shade of the cedars.

And then there was the anxious week when Zephania had a bad sore throat that looked for awhile like diphtheria, and Wade prepared his own breakfasts and lunches and dined alternately at The Cedars and with Doctor Crimmins. And, of course, there was the stirring occasion of Zephania's return to duty, Zephania being patently proud of the disturbance she had created, and full of quaint comments on life, death, and immortality, those subjects seemingly having engaged her mind largely during her illness. For several days her voice was noticeably lacking in quality and volume, and "There is a Happy Land," which was her favorite hymn during that period, was rendered so subduedly that Wade was worried, and had to have the Doctor's assurance that Zephania was not going into a decline.

These are only a few of the exciting things that transpired during Wade's first month in Eden Village. There were many others, but as I tell them they seem much less important than they really were, and I shall mention only one more. That was something other than a mere event; it savored of the stupendous; it might almost be called a phenomenon. Its fame spread abroad until folks discussed it over the tea-table or in front of the village stores in places as far distant as Stepping and Tottingham and Bursley. In Eden Village it caused such a commotion as had not disturbed the tranquillity since the weather-vane on the church steeple was regilded. As you are by this time, kind reader, in a fever of excitement and curiosity, I'll relieve your suspense.

Wade had his cottage painted, inside and out!

Not content with that, he had a new roof put on, built a porch on the south side of the house, cut a door from the sitting-room, and had the fence mended and the gate rehung! It was the consensus of Eden Village opinion that you can't beat a Westerner for extravagance and sheer audacity.

But I haven't told you all even yet. I've saved something for a final thrill. Wade had dormer windows built into the sleeping-rooms, a thing which so altered the appearance of the house that the neighbors stood aghast. Some of the older ones shook their heads and wondered what old Colonel Selden Phelps would say if he could say anything. And the spirit of progress and improvement reached even to the grounds. Zenas Third toiled with spade and pruning-knife and bundles of shrubs and plants came from Boston and were set out with lavish prodigality. In the matter of alterations to the house Eve was consulted on every possible occasion, while garden improvements were placed entirely in Miss Mullett's capable hands. That lady was in her element, and for a week or more one could not pass the cottage without spying Miss Mullett and Zenas Third hard at work somewhere about. Miss Mullett wore a wide-brimmed straw hat to keep the sun from her pink cheeks and a pair of Wade's discarded gloves to save her hands. The gloves were very, very much too large for her, and, when not actually engaged in using her trowel, Miss Mullett stood with arms held out in scarecrow style so as not to contaminate her gown with garden mold, and presented a strange and unusual appearance. Every afternoon, as regular as clockwork, the Doctor came down the street and through the gate to lavish advice, commendation, and appropriate quotations from his beloved poets. At five Zephania appeared with the tea things and the *partie carrée* gathered in the parlor and brought their several little histories up to date, and laughed and poked fun at each other, and drew more and more together as time passed.

Perhaps you've been thinking that Wade's advent in Eden Village was the signal for calls and invitations to dinners, receptions, and bridge. If you have you don't know New England, or, at least, you don't know Eden Village. One can't dive into society in Eden Village; one has to wade in, and very cautiously. In the course of events the newcomer became thoroughly immersed, and the waters of Eden Village society enclosed him beneficently, but that was not yet. He was still undergoing his novitiate, and to raise his hat to Miss Cousins, when he encountered that austere lady on the street, was as yet the height of social triumph. Wade, however, was experiencing no yearnings for a wider social sphere. Eve and Miss Mullett and the Doctor, Zephania, and the two Zenases were sufficient for him. In fact he would have been quite satisfied with one of that number could he have chosen the one.

For Wade's deliberate effort to fall in love with Eve had proved brilliantly successful. In fact he had not been conscious of the effort at all, so simple and easy had the process proved. Of course he ought to have been delighted, but, strange to tell, after the first brief moment of self-gratulation, he began to entertain doubts as to the wisdom of his plan. Regrets succeeded doubts. Being in love with a girl who didn't care a rap whether you stayed or went wasn't the unalloyed bliss he had pictured. He would know better another time.

That was in the earlier stage. Later it dawned upon him that there never could be another time, and he didn't want that there should. This knowledge left him rather dazed. He felt a good deal like a man who, walking across a pleasant beach and enjoying the view, suddenly finds himself up to his neck in quicksand. And, like a person in such a quandary, Wade's first instinctive thought was to struggle.

The struggle lasted three days, three days during which he sedulously avoided The Cedars and tramped dozens of miles with Zenas Third in search of fish—and very frequently lost his bait because his thoughts were busy elsewhere. At the end of the three days he found himself, to return to our comparison, deeper than ever.

Then it was that he looked facts in the face. He reduced the problem to simple quantities and studied it all one evening, with the aid of an eighth of a pound of tobacco and a pile of lumber which the carpenters had left near the woodshed. The problem, as Wade viewed it, was this:

A man, with little to recommend him save money, is head over heels in love with the loveliest, dearest girl the Lord ever made, a girl a thousand times too good for the man, and who doesn't care any more for him than she does for the family cat or the family doctor. What's the answer?

Wade gave it up—the problem, not the girl. He wasn't good at problems. Out West it had been Ed Craig who had figured out the problems on paper, and Wade who had reached the same conclusions with pick and shovel and dynamite. Their methods differed, but the results attained were similar. So, as I have said, Wade abandoned the problem on paper and set to work, metaphorically, with steel and explosives.

XII.

There was a bench outside the kitchen door at The Cedars, a slant-legged, unpainted bench which at one time had been used to hold milk-cans. Wade settled himself on this in company with several dozen glasses of currant jelly. From his position he could look in at the kitchen door upon Eve and Miss Mullett, who, draped from chin to toes in blue-checked aprons, were busy over the summer preserving. A sweet, spicy fragrance was wafted out to him from the bubbling kettles, and now and then Eve, bearing a long agate-ware spoon and adorned on one cheek with a brilliant streak of currant juice, came to the threshold and smiled down upon him in a preoccupied manner, glancing at the jelly tumblers anxiously.

"If you spill them," she said, "Carrie will never forgive you, Mr. Herrick."

"Nonsense," declared Miss Mullett from the kitchen. "I'd just send you for more, Mr. Herrick, and make you help me put them up."

"I think I'd like that," answered Wade.

"It must be rather good fun messing about with sugar and currants and things."

"Messing about!" exclaimed Eve, indignantly. "It's quite evident that you've never done any of it!"

"Well, I stewed some dried apricots once," said Wade, "and they weren't half bad. I suppose you're going to be busy all the morning, aren't you?" he asked, forlornly.

"I'm afraid so."

"Indeed you're not," said Miss Mullett, decisively. "You're going to stop as soon as we get this kettleful off. I can do the rest much better without you, dear."

"Did you ever hear such ingratitude?" laughed Eve. "Here I've been hard at work since goodness only knows what hour of the morning, and now I'm informed that my services are valueless! I shall stay and help just to spite you, Carrie."

"I wanted you to take a walk," said Wade, boldly. "It's a great morning, too fine to be spent indoors."

"Is it?" Eve looked up at the fleecy sky critically. "Don't you think it looks like rain?"

"Not a bit," he answered, stoutly. "We're in for a long drought. Zephania told me so not half an hour ago."

"Is Zephania a weather prophet?"

"She's everything. She knows so much that she makes me ashamed of myself. And she never makes a mistake about the weather."

Wade waited anxiously.

"We-ll," said Eve, finally, "if you're sure it isn't going to rain, and Carrie really doesn't want me—"

"I do not," said Miss Mullett, crisply. "A walk will do you good. She stayed up until all hours last night, Mr. Herrick, writing. I wish you'd say something to her; she pays no attention to me."

Wade flushed. Eve turned and shot an indignant glance at Miss Mullett, but that lady was busy over the kettle with her back toward them.

"I'm afraid she would pay less heed to me than to you," answered Wade with a short laugh. "But if you'll persuade her to walk, I'll lecture her as much as you wish."

"If I'm to be lectured," replied Eve, "I shan't go."

"Well, of course, if you put it that way," hedged Wade.

"Go along, dear," said Miss Mullett. "You need fresh air. But do keep out of the sun if it gets hot."

"I wonder," observed Wade, with a smile, "what you folks up here would do down in New Mexico, where the temperature gets up to a hundred and twenty in the shade."

"I'd do as the Irishman suggested," answered Eve, pertly, "and keep out of the shade. If you'll wait right where you are and not move for ten minutes I'll go and get ready."

"I won't ruffle a feather," Wade assured her. "But you'd better come before dinner time or I may get hungry and eat all the jelly."

Twenty minutes later she was back, a cool vision of white linen and lace. She wore no hat, but had brought a sunshade. Pursued by Miss Mullett's admonitions to keep out of the sun as much as possible, they went down the garden and through the gate, and turned countryward under the green gloom of the elms. Alexander the Great, laboring perhaps under the delusion that he was a dog instead of a cat, followed them decorously for some distance, and then, being prevailed on to desist, climbed a fence-post and blinked gravely after them.

"It really is nice to-day," said Eve. "When the breeze comes from the direction of the coast it cools things off deliciously. I suppose it's only imagination, but sometimes I think I can smell the salt—or taste it. That's scarcely possible, though, for we're a good twenty miles inland."

"I'm not so sure," he answered. "Lots of times I've thought I could smell the ocean here. Does it take very long to get to Portsmouth or the beach? Couldn't we go some day, you and Miss Mullett and the Doctor and I?"

"That would be jolly," said Eve. "We must talk it over with them. I'm afraid, though, the Doctor couldn't go. There's always some one sick hereabouts."

"Oh, he could leave enough of his nasty medicine one day to last through the next. He's one of the nicest old chaps I ever met, Miss Walton. He's awfully fond of you, isn't he?"

"I think he is," she answered, "and I'm awfully fond of him, I don't know whether I ought to tell this, but I have a suspicion that he used to be very fond of my mother before she was married. He's told me so many little things about her, and he always speaks of her in such a quiet, dear sort of way. I wonder—I wonder if he ever asked her to marry him."

"Somehow I don't believe he ever did," said Wade, thoughtfully. "I could imagine him being sort of shy if he were in love. Perhaps, while he was working his courage up to the sticking point, your father stepped in and carried off the prize. That happens sometimes, you know."

"I suppose it does," laughed Eve. "Or perhaps he was so busy quoting bits of poetry to her that he never had time!"

"That's so." Wade smiled. "There's one thing certain, and that is, if she did refuse him, he had a quotation quite ready for the occasion."

"'Tis better to have loved and lost' and so on?"

"Something of the sort," answered Wade. "I wonder, though, if that is true, Miss Walton?"

"What?" asked Eve.

"That it's better to have loved and lost than never to have loved at all."

"I'm sure I don't know. Probably not. Perhaps, like a great many of the Doctor's quotations, it's more poetical than truthful."

"I think it must be," mused Wade. "It doesn't sound logical to me. To say that, when you've seen a thing you want and can't have it, you're better off than before you wanted it, doesn't sound like sense."

"Have you ever wanted much you didn't get?" asked Eve.

Wade thought a minute.

"Come to think of it, Miss Walton, I don't believe I have. I can't think of anything just now. Perhaps that's why I'd hate all the more to be deprived of what I want now," he said, seriously. She shot a glance at him from under the edge of the sunshade.

"You talk as though some one was trying to cheat you out of something you'd set your heart on," she said lightly.

"That isn't far wrong," he answered. "I have set my heart on something and it doesn't look now as though I'd ever get it."

"Oh, I hope you will," said Eve, sincerely.

"Your saying that makes it look farther off than ever," responded Wade, with a wry smile.

"My saying that? But why?" she asked in surprise.

"Because," he answered, after a moment's silence, "if you knew what it is I want, I don't think you'd want me to have it, and that you don't know proves that I'm a long way off from it."

"It sounds like a riddle," said Eve, perplexedly. "Please, Mr. Herrick, what is the answer?"

Wade clenched his hands in his pockets and looked very straight ahead up the road.

"You," he said.

"*Me?*" The sunshade was raised for an instant. "*Oh!*" The sunshade dropped. They walked on in silence for a few paces. Then said Wade, with a stolen glance at the white silken barrier:

"I hope I haven't offended you, Miss Walton. I had no more intention of saying anything like that when we started out than—than the man in the moon. But it's true, and you might as well know it now as any other time. You're what I want, more than I've ever wanted anything before or ever shall again, and you're what I'm very much afraid I won't get. I'm not quite an idiot, after all. I know mighty well that—that I'm not the sort of fellow you'd fall in love with, barring a miracle. But maybe I'm trusting to the miracle. Anyhow, I'm cheeky enough to hope that—that you may get to like me enough to marry me some day. Do you think you ever could?"

"But—oh, I don't know what to say," cried Eve, softly. "I haven't thought —!"

"Of course not," interrupted Wade, cheerfully. "Why should you? All I ask is that you think about it now—or some time when you—when you're not busy, you know. I guess I could say a whole lot about how much I love you, but you're not ready to hear that yet and I won't. If you'll just understand that you're the one girl in the whole darn—in the whole world for me, Miss Walton, we'll let it go at that for the present. You think about it. I'm not much on style and looks, and I don't know much outside of mining, but I pick up things pretty quickly and I could learn. I don't say anything about money, except that if you cared for me I'd be thankful I had plenty of it, so that I could give you most anything you wanted. You—you don't mind thinking it over, do you?"

"No," said Eve, a little unsteadily, "but—oh, I do wish you wouldn't talk as you do! You make me feel so little and worthless, and I don't like to feel that way."

"But how?" cried Wade, in distress. "I don't mean to!"

"I know you don't. That's just it. But you do. When you talk so meanly of yourself, I mean. Just as though any girl wouldn't feel proud at having—at hearing—oh, you must know what I mean!" And Eve turned a flushed, beseeching face toward him.

"Not quite, I'm afraid," Wade answered. "Anyhow, I don't want you to feel proud, Miss Walton. If any one should feel proud, it's I, to think you've let me say this to you and haven't sent me off about my business."

"Oh, please!" begged Eve, with a little vexed laugh.

"What?" he asked, perplexedly.

"Don't talk of yourself as though you were—were just nothing, and of me as though I were a princess. It's absurd! I'm only a very ordinary sort of person with ordinary faults—perhaps more than my share of them."

"You're the finest woman I ever saw, and the loveliest," replied Wade stoutly. "And if you're not for me no other woman is."

The sunshade intervened again and they walked on for some little distance in silence. Then Wade began slowly, choosing his words: "Maybe I've talked in a way to give you a wrong impression. You mustn't think that there's any—false modesty about me. I reckon I have rather too good an opinion of myself, if anything. I wouldn't want you to be disappointed in me—afterwards, you know. I reckon I've got an average amount of sense and ability. I've been pretty successful for a man of twenty-eight, and it hasn't been all luck, not by a whole lot! Maybe most folks would say I was conceited, had a swelled head. It's only when it comes to—to asking you to marry me that I get kind of down on myself. I know I'm not good enough, Miss Walton, and I own up to it. The only comforting thought is that there aren't many men who are. I'm saying this because I don't want to fool you into thinking me any more modest and humble than I am. You understand?"

"Yes, I understand," replied Eve, from under the sunshade.

"And you won't forget your promise?"

"You mean—"

"To think it over."

"No, I won't forget. But please don't hope too much, Mr. Herrick, for I can't promise anything, really! It isn't that I don't like you, for I do, but"—her voice trailed off into silence.

"I hardly dared hope for that much," said Wade, gratefully. "Of course it isn't enough, but it's something to start on."

"But liking isn't love," objected Eve, gravely.

"I know. And there was never love without liking. You don't mind if I get what comfort I can out of that, do you?"

"N-no, I suppose not," answered Eve, slowly.

"It doesn't bind you to anything, you see. Shall we turn back now? The breeze seems to have left us."

Presently he said: "There's something I want very much to ask you, but I don't know whether I have any right to."

"If there's anything I can answer, I will," said Eve.

"Then I'll ask it, and you can do as you please about answering. It's just this. Is there anyone who has—a prior claim? I mean is there any one you must consider in this, Miss Walton. Please don't say a word unless you want to."

Eve made no reply for a moment. Then, "I think I'm glad you did ask that, Mr. Herrick," she said, "for it gives me a chance to explain why I haven't answered you this morning, instead of putting it off. I am not bound in any way by any promise of mine, and yet—there is some one who—I hardly know how to put it, Mr. Herrick."

"Don't try if it is too hard. I think I understand."

"I don't believe you do, though. I'm not quite sure—it's only this; that I want to feel quite free before—I answer you. I may have to keep you waiting for awhile, perhaps a few days. May I? You won't mind?"

"I can wait for a year as long as waiting means hope," replied Wade, gravely.

"But maybe—it doesn't."

"But it does. If there was no hope, absolutely none, you'd have told me so ten minutes ago, wouldn't you?"

"I suppose so. I don't know. I mean"—she stopped and faced him, half laughing, half serious. "Oh, I don't know what I mean; you've got me all mixed up! Please, let's not talk any more about it now. Let's—let's go home!"

"Very well," said Wade, cheerfully. "I hope I haven't walked you too far."

XIII.

After supper that night Wade called on Doctor Crimmins. The Doctor occupied a small house which had many years before been used as a school. At one side the Doctor had built a little office, with an entrance from a short brick walk leading to the street. The ground-glass door held the inscription, "Josiah L. Crimmins, M.D. Office." Wade's ring brought the Doctor's housekeeper, a bent, near-sighted, mumbling old woman, who informed Wade that the Doctor was out on a call, but would be back presently. She led the way into the study, turned up the lamp and left him. The study was office and library and living-room in one, a large, untidy room with books lining two sides of it, and a third devoted to shelf on shelf of bottles and jars and boxes. Near the bottle end of the apartment the Doctor had his desk and his few appliances. At the other end was a big oak table covered with a debris of books, magazines, newspapers, tobacco cans, pipes, and general litter. There was a mingled odor, not unpleasant, of drugs and disinfectants, tobacco and leather. Wade made himself comfortable in a big padded armchair, one of those genuinely comfortable chairs which modern furnishers have thrust into oblivion, picked up a magazine at random, slapped the dust off it and filled his pipe. He was disturbed by the sound of brisk footsteps on the bricks outside. Then a key was inserted in the lock and the Doctor entered from the little lobby, bag in hand.

"Ha! Who have we here? Welcome, my dear Herrick, welcome! I hope you come as a friend and not as a patient. Quite right, sir. Keep out of the doctor's clutches as long as possible. Well, well, a warm night this." The Doctor wiped his face with his handkerchief, wafting a strong odor of ether about the room. Then he took off his black frock-coat, hung it on a hook behind the door, and slipped into a rusty old brown velvet house-coat. After that he filled his pipe, talking the while, and, when it was lighted, said "Ha" again very loudly and contentedly, and took down a half-gallon bottle from the medicine shelves. This he placed on the table by the simple expedient of sweeping a pile of newspapers to the floor.

"Now where are those glasses, I wonder?" He looked about the room searchingly over the tops of his spectacles. "There we are." He discovered one on his desk and another on the shelf over the little sink. The latter held some liquid which he first smelled, then tasted and finally threw away. "Wonder what that was," he muttered. "Well, a little rinsing will fix it. Here we are now, Mr. Herrick. Pour your drink, sir, and I'll put the water in. Don't be afraid of it. It's as mild as milk."

"You're quite sure it isn't laudanum?" asked Wade, with a suspicious look at the big bottle.

"Bless you, no." The Doctor lowered himself into a chair with a sigh of relief and contentment. "Now tell me the news, Mr. Herrick. I haven't seen our good friends at The Cedars since yesterday."

Wade sipped from his glass, set it down, hesitated.

"The only piece of news I have, Doctor," he said, finally, "is that I asked Miss Walton to marry me this morning."

"Bless my soul!" The Doctor started to rise. "I do most heartily congratulate you, Mr. Herrick!"

"Hold on, though," said Wade. "Don't jump to conclusions. She hasn't accepted me, Doctor."

"What! But she's going to?"

"I wish I was certain," replied Wade, with a smile.

"But—why, I'd have said she was fond of you, Mr. Herrick. Miss Mullett and I were talking it over just the other day. Old busy-bodies, I suppose you'd call us. But what did she say—if that isn't an impertinent question, sir."

"Well, it seems that there's some one else."

"Never!"

"Yes. I don't know why there shouldn't be."

"Miss Mullett told me that Miss Eve had never shown the slightest favor to any one since she'd known her."

"Maybe this was before that. It isn't very clear just how the other chap stands with her. But she asked time to think it over."

The Doctor chuckled. "Who hesitates is lost, Mr. Herrick. Take my word for it,—she'll come around before long. I'm very glad. She's a fine woman, a fine woman. I knew her mother."

"Well, I hope you're right, Doctor. Maybe you'd better not say anything about it just yet."

"Not a word, sir. I presume, though, if you do marry her, you'll take her out West with you."

"I don't dare make plans yet. I'm sure, though, we'd come to Eden Village in the summer."

"I hope so. I wouldn't want to think I wasn't to see her again. I'm very fond of her in an old man's way. How is the house getting along? Workmen almost through, I guess."

"They've promised to get out to-morrow. And that reminds me, Doctor. I want the ladies and you to take dinner with me Saturday night. It's to be a sort of house-warming, you know. Mrs. Prout is coming over to cook for me and Zephania is to serve. I may depend on you?"

"To be sure, sir. I'll just make a note of it. Saturday, you said? H'm, yes, Saturday. About half-past six, I presume?" The Doctor pulled himself from his chair and rummaged about his desk. "Well, I can't ... seem to ... find my ... memorandum, but I'll remember without it. You—ah—you might mention it to me again in a day or two. I hope by that time we'll be able to drink a toast, sir, to you and Miss Eve."

"You don't hope so any more than I do," said Wade gravely. "I only wish —" He stopped, frowned at his pipe and went on. "The devil of it is, Doctor, I feel so confoundedly cheeky."

"Eh?"

"I mean about asking her to marry a fellow like me."

"What's the matter with you? You're of sound body and mind, aren't you?"

"Yes, I reckon so. But I'm such a useless sort, in a way. I've never done anything except make some money."

"Some women would think you'd done quite enough," replied the Doctor, dryly.

"But she's not that sort. I don't believe she cares anything about money. I've been trying to get her to let me do the square thing with Ed's property, but she won't listen."

"Wanted to parcel some of it out to her, eh? Well, I guess Eve wouldn't have it."

"No, she wouldn't. She ought to, too. It should have been hers, by rights. If it wasn't for that silly quarrel between her father and Ed's—"

"I know, I know. But she's right, according to her lights, Mr. Herrick. Irv Walton wouldn't have touched any of that money with a pair of pincers. Still, I don't see as you need to have such a poor opinion of yourself. We can't all be great generals or statesmen or financiers. Some of us have to wear the drab. And, after all, it doesn't matter tuppence what you are, Mr. Herrick, if you've got the qualities that appeal to Eve. Lord love us! Where would civilization be if it was only the famous men who found wives? I don't think any the worse of myself, Mr. Herrick, because I've never made the world sit up and take notice. I've had my battles and victories, and I don't despise them because there was no waving of flags or sounding of trumpets. I've lived clean—as clean as human flesh may, I guess,—I've been true to my friends and honest to my enemies, and here I am, as good as the next man, to my own thinking."

"I dare say you're right," answered Wade, "but when you love a woman, you sort of want to have a few trophies handy to throw down at her feet, if you see what I mean. You'd like to say, 'Look, I've done this and that! I've conquered here and there! I am Somebody!'"

"And if she didn't love you she'd turn up her nose at your trophies, and like as not walk off with the village fool."

"Well, but it seems to me that a woman isn't likely to love a man unless he has something to show besides a pocketbook."

"Mr. Herrick, there's just one reason why a woman loves a man, and that's because she loves him. You can invent all the theories you want, and you can write tons of poetry about it, and when you get through you'll be just where you started. You can find a reason for pretty near everything a woman does, though you may have to rack your brains like the devil to do it, but you can't explain why she falls in love with this man and not with that. Perhaps you recall Longfellows's lines: 'The men that women marry, and why they marry them, will always be a marvel and a mystery to the world.' Personally, I'm a bit of a fatalist regarding love. I think hearts are mated when they're fashioned, and when they get together you can no more keep them apart than you keep two drops of quicksilver from running into each other when they touch. It's as good a theory as any, for it can't be disproved."

"Then how account for unhappy marriages?" asked Wade.

"I said hearts were mated, not bodies and brains, nor livers, either. Half the unhappy marriages are due, I dare say, to bad livers."

"Well," laughed Wade, rising and finding his hat, "your theory sounds reasonable. As for me, I have no theory—nor data. So I'll go home and go to sleep. Don't forget Saturday night, Doctor."

"Saturday night? Oh, to be sure, to be sure. I'll not forget, you may depend. Good night, Mr. Herrick, and thank you for looking in on me. And—ah—Mr. Herrick?"

"Yes?"

"Ah—I wouldn't be too meek, if I were you. Even Fate may relish a little assistance. Good night. I wouldn't be surprised if we had a thunder storm before morning."

XIV.

Wade was relieved to find that Eve's manner toward him had undergone no change by reason of his impromptu declaration. They met quite as before, and if there was any embarrassment on the part of either of them it was not on hers. During the next few days it happened that he seldom found himself alone with her for more than a few moments, but it did not occur to him that Chance alone was not responsible. As Wade understood it, it was a period of truce, and he was careful not to give word or look that might be construed into a violation of terms. Perhaps he overdid it a little, for there were times, usually when he was not looking, when Eve shot speculating, slightly puzzled glances at him. Perhaps she was thinking that such subjects as last night's thunder storm, dormer windows, and the apple crop outlook were not just what a declared lover might be supposed to choose for conversation. Once or twice, notably toward the end of the week, and when she had been presumably making up her mind for three days, she exhibited signs of irritability and impatience. These Wade construed as evidences of boredom and acted upon as such, cheerfully taking himself off.

The house-warming, as Wade chose to call his dinner-party, came off on Saturday night. Wade had moved his bed back to the guest-room upstairs and the sitting-room had regained its former character. In this room and in the parlor and dining-room bowls and vases of pink roses—which had come from Boston on ice in great wooden boxes, and about which the village at large was already excitedly speculating—stood in every available spot. But if Eden Village found subject for comment in the extravagant shipment of roses, imagine its wonderment when it beheld, shortly after six o'clock, Doctor Crimmins parading magnificently up the street in swallow-tailed coat and white vest, a costume which Miss Cousins was certain he had not worn in twenty years!

Wade and his guests sat on the new side porch while awaiting dinner and Wade came in for a lot of praise for the improvements he had worked in his garden, praise which he promptly disclaimed in favor of Miss Mullett.

"Goodness only knows what I'd have done if it hadn't been for her," he laughed. "I wanted to plant American Beauty roses and maiden-hair fern all over the place. I even think I had some notion of growing four-dollar orchids on the pear trees. The idea of putting in things that would really grow was entirely hers."

"I like the idea of planting the old-fashioned, hardy things," said the Doctor. "They're the best, after all. Asters and foxgloves and deutzia and snowballs and all the rest of them."

"And phlox," said Wade. "They told us we were planting too late, but the phlox has buds on it already. Come and see it."

So they trooped down the new gray steps and strolled around the garden, Wade exhibiting proudly and miscalling everything, and Miss Mullett gently correcting him.

Their travels took them around the house and finally to the gate in the hedge, over the arch of which Miss Mullett was coaxing climbing roses. When they turned back Eve and the Doctor walked ahead.

"Eve told me once such a quaint thing about that gate," said Miss Mullett. "It seems that when she was a little girl and used to play in the garden over there, she imagined all sorts of queer things, as children will. And one of them was that some day a beautiful prince would come through the gate in the hedge and fall on his knee and ask her to marry him. Such a quaint idea for a child to have, wasn't it?"

"Yes," answered Wade thoughtfully. There was silence for a moment, and then he glanced down and met Miss Mullett's gaze. He laughed ruefully.

"Do you think I look much like a prince?" he asked.

"Do looks matter," she said, gently, "if you *are* the prince?"

"Perhaps not, but—I'm afraid I'm not."

Thereupon Miss Mullett did a most unmaidenly thing. She found Wade's hand and pressed it with her cool, slim fingers.

"If I were a prince," she replied, "I'd be afraid of nothing."

There was just time to return the pressure of her hand and give a grateful look into the kindly face, and then they were back with the others on the porch.

That dinner was an immense success from every standpoint, Mrs. Prout cooked like *cordon bleu*, Zephania, all starch and frills and excitement, served like a—but no, she didn't; she served in a manner quite her own, bringing on the oysters with a whispered aside to Wade that she had "most forgot the ice," introducing the chicken with a triumphant laugh, and standing off to observe the effect it made before returning to the kitchen for the new potatoes, late asparagus, and string-beans, so tiny that Mrs. Prout declared it was a sin and a shame to pick them. There was a salad of lettuce and tomatoes, and the Doctor, with grave mien, prepared the dressing, tasting it at every stage and uttering congratulatory "Ha's!" And there were plenty of strawberries and much cake— Zephania's very best maple-layer—and ice-cream from Manchester, a trifle soft, but, as Eve maintained, all the better when you put it over the berries. And—breathe it softly lest Eden Village hear—there was champagne! Eve and Miss Mullett treated it with vast respect, but the Doctor met it metaphorically with open arms, as one welcomes an old friend, and, under its gentle influence, tossed aside twenty years and made decorous, but desperate, love to Miss Mullett. And then, to continue the pleasant formality of the occasion, the ladies withdrew to the parlor, and Wade and the Doctor smoked two very stout and very black cigars and sipped two tiny glasses of brandy.

In the parlor Miss Mullett turned to Eve in excited trepidation. "My dear," she asked, in a thrilling whisper, "*do* you think I took too much champagne? My cheeks are positively burning!"

"I don't know," laughed Eve, "but the color is very becoming, dear."

"But I shouldn't want Mr. Herrick to think—"

"He won't," replied Eve, soothingly. "No matter how intoxicated you got, I'm sure he is too much of a gentleman to think any such thing."

"Any such thing as what?"

"Why, what you said."

"But I hadn't said!" declared Miss Mullett, sinking tragically onto the couch. Whereupon Eve laughed, and Miss Mullett declared that rather than have the gentleman think her the least bit—well—the very least bit, you understand!—she would go right home. And Eve was forced to assure her with serious face that she wasn't the least bit, and wasn't in any danger of becoming so. Miss Mullett was comforted and Eve, who had been standing by the marble-topped table, idly opened a book lying there. It wasn't a very interesting volume, from her point of view, being a work on metallurgy. She turned to the front and found Wade's name written on the fly-leaf, and was about to lay it down when she caught sight of a piece of paper marking a place. With no thought of prying, she opened the book again. The paper proved to be an empty envelope addressed to Wade in typewritten characters. In the upper left-hand corner was an inscription that interested her: "After five days return to The Evelyn Mining Co., Craig's Camp, Colo."

She studied the words for a long minute. Then she smiled and closed the book again. Oddly enough, both she and Wade had discovered each other's secrets that evening.

When the men joined them the Doctor suggested whist. Wade protested his stupidity, but was overruled and assigned to Miss Mullett as partner.

"If you played like John Hobb," declared the Doctor, "you'd win with Miss Mullett for partner."

Eve and Wade desired to know who John Hobb was, and the Doctor was forced to acknowledge him a quite mythical character, whose name in that part of the world stood proverbially for incompetence. After that when any of the four made a mistake he or she was promptly dubbed John Hobb. For once the unwritten law was unobserved, and it was long past ten when the party broke up, Eve and the Doctor having captured the best of a series of rubbers. After they had gone Wade put out the downstair lights and returned to the side porch, where, with his pipe flaring fitfully in the moonlit darkness, he lived over in thought the entire evening and conjured up all sorts of pictures of Eve. When he finally went to bed his last waking sensation was one of gratitude toward Miss Mullett for the words she had spoken in the garden.

The next morning Eve was out under the cedars when the Doctor came marching down the street, carrying his bag and swinging his cane, his lips moving a little with the thoughts that came to him. Opposite Eve's retreat he stood on tiptoes and smiled across the hedge, unseen. She made a pretty picture there over her book, her brown hair holding golden-bronze glints where the sun kissed it, and her smooth cheek warmly pallid in the shade.

"'Old as I am, for ladies' love unfit,
The power of beauty I remember yet,'"

quoted the Doctor. "Good morning, fair Eve of Eden. And how do you find yourself to-day? For my part I am haunted by a gentle, yet insistent, regret." The Doctor placed a hand over his heavy gold watch-chain. "It is here."

"Better there than here," laughed Eve, touching her forehead.

The Doctor pretended affront. "Do you mean to insinuate, young lady, that I drank too much of the wine last night? Ha! I deny it; emphatically I deny it. Besides, one couldn't drink too much of such wine as that! To prove how steady my hand and brain are, I'll come in a moment and talk with you."

The Doctor entered through the gate and advanced toward Eve, who with anxious solicitude cautioned him against colliding with the trees or walking over the flower-beds. Things had changed in the cedars' shade, and now there were three rustic chairs and an ancient iron table there. The Doctor sat himself straightly in one of the chairs and glared at Eve.

"Now what have you to say?" he demanded.

"That you conceal it beautifully," she replied, earnestly.

"Madam, I have nothing to conceal."

"Oh, well, if you persist! Where are you off to this morning?"

"Mother Turner's."

"Is she ill?"

"Probably not. I think myself she's too old to ever be really ill any more. At ninety-eight the body is too well seasoned to admit disease. She will just run peacefully down like a clock some day."

"Does she still smoke her pipe, Doctor?"

"All day long, I think. I remonstrated with her once ten or fifteen years ago when she had a touch of pleurisy. 'Mrs. Turner,' I said, 'if you persist in smoking, you'll injure your health and die young.' She was then eighty-something. 'Doctor,' said she, with a twinkle in those bright little eyes of hers, 'I'll live to be a hundred, and that's more than you'll do.' And, bless me, I think she will! To-day she sent word for me to 'look in.' That means that she needs gossip and not medicine. Well, I'm glad to go. It always does me good to talk with Mother Turner. She's the best lesson in contentment I know. She's buried two husbands, seven children, and the dear Lord only knows how many grandchildren, she lives on charity and hasn't a soul near her she can claim relationship to, and she's as cheerful as that oriole up there, and almost as bright. The pathetic part of it is that she can't read any more, although she puts on her spectacles and pretends that she can. Three years ago she confided to me that her eyesight was 'failing a bit.' She's not blind yet, by any means, but print's beyond her. And so when I see her she always gets me to read to her a little, explaining that her eyes 'be a bit watery this morning.' Sometimes it's the Bible, but more often it's a newspaper that some one has left. Just now her hobby is airships. She can't hear enough about airships." The Doctor chuckled. "She's been on a train but once in her life, she tells me, and that was thirty years ago."

"I don't want to live that long," said Eve thoughtfully. "I don't want to live after every one I've cared for has gone."

"So you think now," replied the Doctor, with a faint shrug of his shoulders, "but wait till you are old. I've seen many snuffed out, my dear, but there's only one or two I recall who went willingly. The love of life is a strong passion. Bless my soul, what's that?"

The Doctor turned toward the lilac hedge and the neighboring cottage, listening. Eve laughed, merrily.

"Why, that's Zephania," she said.

"'We shall sleep, but not forever,
There will be a glorious dawn!
We shall meet to part, no, never,
On the resurrection morn!'"

sang Zephania, in her piping voice. The Doctor smiled. Then he nodded sideways in the direction of the voice.

"Have you seen our host this morning?" he asked.

"No," said Eve.

"I wonder," he chuckled, "if I hadn't better go over and administer a bromide. These fashionable dinner-parties—" He shook his head eloquently.

"I don't believe he's that bad," responded Eve. "I wish you'd tell me what you think of him, Doctor."

"Mr. Herrick? Well, aside from his intemperance—"

"No, I'm in earnest, please. Afterwards I'll tell you why I ask—perhaps."

"I think him a very nice young man, Miss Eve, don't you?"

"Ye-es."

"I wouldn't call him strictly handsome; he doesn't remind me of the copper-engraved pictures of Lord Byron, who, when I was a lad, was considered the standard of masculine beauty, but he looks like a man, which is something that Byron didn't, to my thinking."

"But do you—do you think he's sincere?"

"Lord, bless me, yes! I'd stake my word on his being that if nothing else."

"Even if he is a mining man?" asked Eve, with a smile.

"H'm, well, I guess there are honest mining men as well as honest lawyers."

"Yes, I think he's honest," said Eve, thoughtfully, "but as to sincerity—"

"Aren't they the same?"

"Perhaps they are," answered Eve, doubtfully. She was silent for a moment, possibly considering the question. Then she looked across at the Doctor with a little flush in her cheeks. "You see," she said, "he—he's asked me to marry him."

The Doctor rolled his cane under his palms and nodded his head slowly several times. Eve waited. At last—

"You don't seem much surprised," she said, questioningly.

"Surprised? No. I'd have been surprised if he hadn't asked you to marry him, my dear. It's what I'd have done in his place."

"And I'd have accepted you," said Eve with a little laugh.

"And him?" asked the Doctor.

Eve was silent, looking across the garden. Finally she shrugged her slim shoulders and sighed.

"I don't know," she said, frankly.

"Well," began the Doctor, slowly and judicially. Then he stopped, wondering what he had started to say.

"Why should I?" challenged Eve, a trifle querulously.

"You shouldn't, unless you feel that you want to."

"But I don't know whether I want to—or don't want to."

The Doctor studied her face a moment, until her eyes dropped and the flush deepened in her cheeks. Unseen of her, he smiled.

"Take plenty of time to find out," said the Doctor, softly and kindly. "Don't marry him until you are sure that you can't be happy without him, my dear. Don't try it as an experiment. That's what makes unhappy marriages; at least, that's one thing. There are others too numerous to mention. There's just one reason why a man and a woman should join themselves together in matrimony, and that is love, the love that the poets sing and the rest of us poke fun at, the love that is the nearest thing to Heaven we find on earth." The Doctor sat silent a moment, looking past the girl's grave face into the green blur of the garden. Then he stirred, sighed, and looked at his watch. "Well, well, I must be on my way," he said briskly. "I'm a vastly busy old man."

"But, Doctor, you haven't helped me a bit to decide," she said, aggrievedly.

"I can't, my dear. No one can. And, what's more, you don't want me to."

"Why, Doctor, I"—she began. Then she dropped her eyes and a little smile trembled at her lips. "How do you know?" she asked.

"I know a few things yet, Miss Eve," he chuckled, picking up his old black leather bag.

"Just a moment, please," begged Eve. "Did he ever tell you that he wanted me to take some of Cousin Edward's money?"

"M'm, yes, he did tell me that," responded the Doctor cautiously. "But that's nothing against him."

"N-no, I know it isn't. And he said—says he will have his way."

The Doctor settled his hat and gripped his stick.

"Then I guess he will. He looks that kind of a man."

"He never will," said Eve, firmly, "never!"

"Unless," chuckled the Doctor, "you marry him." He waved his cane and strode away toward the gate. "How about that?" he called back over the hedge.

Eve made no answer. She was thinking very busily. "Unless I marry him!" she repeated, somewhat blankly, staring at the turquoise ring which she was slipping around and around on her finger. The moments passed. A frown crept into her forehead and grew there, dark and threatening, under the warm shadow of her hair. "And so that's it," she thought bitterly and angrily. "That's what it means. That's why he's acted so strangely since—since he asked me to marry him. It's just a trick to get his own way. He'd marry me as a sop to his conscience. It's just the money, after all. Oh, I wish—I wish Cousin Edward had never had any money!"

She sat there a long time, while the shadows shortened and the birds grew silent, one by one, and the noonday hush fell over the old garden;

sat there until Miss Mullett came to the kitchen door and summoned her to luncheon.

XV.

Wade rolled a vest into a tight wad and tucked it into a corner of the till. Then he glanced around the sitting-room, saw nothing else to pack, and softly dropped the lid. That done he sat down on it and relighted his pipe.

It was two days since Eve and the Doctor had talked under the cedars, one day since Wade had received her note. He had not seen her since. She hadn't asked him not to, but Wade had stereotyped ideas as to the proper conduct of a rejected suitor, and he intended to live up to them. Of course he would call in the morning and say good bye.

He felt no resentment against Eve, although her note would have supplied sufficient excuse. He didn't quite know what he did feel. He had striven the evening before to diagnose his condition, with the result that he had decided that his heart was not broken, although there was a peculiar dull aching sensation there that he fancied was destined to grow worse before it got better. So far, what seemed to trouble him most was leaving the cottage and Eden Village. He had grown very fond of both. Already they seemed far more like home to him than Craig's Camp or any place he had known. There had been nothing in that brief, unsatisfactory note intimating that he was expected to leave Eden Village, but he was quite sure that his departure would be the best thing for all concerned. The Doctor, to whom he had confided his plan, had thought differently, and had begged him to wait and see if things didn't change. The Doctor was a mighty good sort, but—well, he hadn't read Eve's note!

He wasn't leaving Eden Village for good and all. There was comfort in that thought. Some day, probably next summer, he would come back. By that time he would have gotten over it in all probability. Until such time Mr. Zenas Prout and Zephania, in fact the whole Prout family, there to take care of the cottage. Zephania was to sweep it once a month from top to bottom. Wade smiled. He hadn't suggested such care as that, but Zephania had insisted. Zephania, he reflected with a feeling of gratitude, had been rather cut up about his departure.

Of course it was nobody's fault but his own. He had deliberately fallen in love, scorning consequences. Now he was staring at the consequences and didn't like their looks. Thank Heaven, he was a worker, and there was plenty of work to do. Whitehead and the others out there would be surprised to see him coming into camp again so soon. Well, that was nothing. Perhaps, too, it was just as well he was going back early. There was the new shaft-house to get up, and the sooner that was ready the sooner they could work the new lead. He raised his head, conscious of a disturbing factor, and then arose and closed the door into the hall. Closing the door muffled the strains that floated down from upstairs, where Zephania, oppressed, but defiant of sorrow, was singing:

"'My days are gliding swiftly by,
And I, a pilgrim stranger,
Would not detain them as they fly!
Those hours of toil and danger.'"

After awhile, his pipe having gone out again from neglect, he strapped and locked the trunk, glanced at his watch and took up his hat. He passed out through the immaculate kitchen, odorous of soapsuds and sunlight, and down through the orchard, which Zenas Third with his saw and shears had converted from a neglected and scrubby riot into a spruce and orderly parade. Unconsciously his feet led him over the same course he had taken on that first walk of his, which ended in an unintentional and disconcerting visit to The Cedars. As before, he followed the brook, much less a brook now than then by reason of the summer drought, and speculated as to the presence of fish therein. He had intended all along to stroll down here some day and try for sunfish, but he had never done it. Well, that was one of several dreamed-of things which had not come to pass.

The meadow grass had grown tall and heavy, and was touched with gold and russet where the afternoon sunlight slanted across it. The birds flew up at his approach and scattered in darts and circles. To-day when he reached the fence he didn't turn aside toward the road, but climbed over and found an open space on the side of the little hill under the trees, and threw himself down there to smoke his pipe and stare back across the meadow. It was very still in the woods, with only the sleepy chirp of a bird or rustling of a squirrel to be heard, but from somewhere in the hot glare of the afternoon came the rasping of the first locust.

Zephania served supper that evening with chastened mien, and for once she neglected to sing.

"You do think you'll come back, don't you, Mr. Herrick?" she asked.

"Why, yes, Zephania, I expect to. Do you want me to?"

"Oh, yes, sir! We all want you to. Father says if there was more gentlemen like you here, Eden Village would perk right up. And Zenas says you and he haven't done nearly all the fishing you were going to."

"No, I suppose not. Tell him we'll try again next summer. I'm leaving my tackle here, tell him, so as I will be sure to come back."

"Yes, sir." Zephania hesitated, half-way to the door. Finally, "It's been awful nice for me, Mr. Herrick," she said. "I've had just the best summer I ever did have."

"Why, you've had a lot of hard work," said Wade. "Is that what you call nice?"

"Yes, sir, but it ain't been very hard. I like to work. It seems as though the harder I work the happier I am, Mr. Herrick."

"Really? Well, now, I reckon that's the way with me, Zephania, come to think about it. I suppose keeping busy at something you like doing comes just as near to spelling happiness as anything can, eh?"

"Yes sir."

"By the way, Zephania, do you wear a hat?"

"Why, yes, sir, of course!"

"Oh! Well, I didn't know; I never saw you with one on. How would you like me to send you a hatpin, then, with a nice little gold nugget for a head?"

"I'd love it! But—but what is a nugget, Mr. Herrick?"

"Oh, a little—a little lump."

"Do you mean real gold?" asked Zephania, awedly.

"Yes, real gold, virgin gold, just as it comes out of the ground, you know."

"Wouldn't it be worth a good deal, though?" asked Zephania, doubtfully.

"Oh, a few dollars; ten or fifteen. Why?"

"I'd almost be afraid of losing it, Mr. Herrick. Would you please see that it wasn't a very big nug—nug—"

"Nugget'? All right," he laughed. "I'll see that it's only about as big as your thumbnail."

"Thank you, sir; I'd think a great deal of it. Will you have some more tea?"

"No, no more tea, Zephania. No more anything. You may take the things out."

Later in the evening came Doctor Crimmins, very regretful and full of arguments in favor of postponing action. When twilight passed they went out onto the porch with their pipes and glasses. They talked as friends talk on the eve of parting, often of trivial things, with long pauses between. The moon came up over the tree tops, round and full, and flooded the garden with silver.

"'The moon, serene in glory, mounts the sky,'" murmured the Doctor. "'The wandering moon'—how does it go? I'm thinking of some lines of Milton's. Let me see; ah!"

"'The wandering moon,
Riding near her highest noon,
Like one that has been led astray
Through the heaven's wide pathless way.'"

Later, when the lights of the village had disappeared one by one under the tranquil elms, the Doctor returned to the attack.

"Take another week to think it over, Herrick," he urged. "Who knows what may happen in a week, eh? Women's minds have been known to change before this, my friend."

"Hers won't," answered Wade, convincedly. "Her note left little doubt as to that."

"But don't you think you ought to see her again?"

"Yes, I shall call in the morning to say good-by."

"H'm, yes," muttered the other, doubtfully. "I know what such a call is like. You go into the parlor and Miss Eve and Miss Mullett come in together, and you all talk a lot of pasty foolishness for five minutes and then you shake hands and leave. That doesn't help any. See her alone if only for a minute, Herrick; give yourselves a chance; bless my soul, lad, don't you realize that you can't risk spoiling two lives for the want of a moment's determination? If it's pride, put it in your pocket!"

"I'd do anything," replied Wade, with a little laugh, "if I thought it could do any good. The fact is, Doctor, I'm pretty certain that the other fellow is too strong for me."

"The other fellow! I don't believe there is or has been another fellow! I'd bet my bottom dollar that you two young folks care for each other. You've gone and made a mess of things between you, and damned if I don't think it's my duty to meddle!"

"Please don't," said Wade. "It's good of you to want to help, but—what's the use of talking about it? Miss Walton knows her own mind—"

"She didn't a couple of days ago," said the Doctor, gruffly. "She asked my advice about you. I told her to take you if she wanted you, and she said she didn't know whether she did or didn't."

"She seems to have found out since then," said Wade, dryly.

"It must have been sudden, then. Look here, was there any quarrel? Any misunderstanding?"

"None. I haven't spoken to her since Saturday night."

"Well, it beats me," said the Doctor, leaning over to knock the ashes from his pipe. "I'm plumb certain she cares for you, and just as certain that you're making a mistake by running away." He stood up and scowled fiercely at the moon. "Well, I must be off. I'll see you to-morrow. You're not going until afternoon, you said?"

"I leave here about two," said Wade. "I shall spend to-morrow night in Boston and take a morning train west."

"Well, you know my opinion," the Doctor growled. "Sleep on it; think it over again. Good night."

After the Doctor had gone Wade sat for a while longer on the porch. He didn't feel the least bit sleepy, and the Doctor had shaken his determination in spite of himself. Supposing, after all—then he shook his head and sighed. There was the note. He fumbled in his pocket and found it and looked at it in the moonlight. There was no use in imagining things when that sheet of paper stared him in the face. He strove to reread the message, but the light was too faint. He folded it again, started to drop it back in his pocket, hesitated, and then tore it savagely into tiny bits and tossed it over the side of the porch. It was as though he had destroyed a malign influence, for, even as the little white fragments went floating down into the shadow, a new hope crept into his heart, and he went upstairs, arguing this way and that in a sudden fever of mental energy. In the bedroom there was no need to light his lamp, and he started to undress in the broad path of moonlight that flooded the little chamber. But after he had thrown his coat aside he forgot to go on with the process, and after many minutes he found himself leaning on the sill of the open window staring at the moon.

"Bed?" he muttered, in a strange excitement. "Why should I go to bed? I'm not sleepy. I'm moon-struck, probably. I'm full of crazy thoughts and fancies. I don't want to sleep, I want to walk—and think. I want to be out of doors."

He found his way down the stairs, unmindful of the fact that he had left his coat behind, and stepped out into the warm fragrant night. The road was a dark cavern, splotched with silver. He turned away from it, seeking the open spaces of the garden, his shadow stalking beside him, purple-black in the moonlight. The air scarcely moved.

The world was hushed and heavy with sleep. Once, as he passed under the drooping branches of a tree, a bird stirred in its nest with a sleepy *cheep*. He made his way around the house at the back, absentmindedly feeling for his coat pocket and his pipe. He had left it upstairs, but no matter. Why should one want to defile such a night as this with tobacco-smoke, anyway? He stopped once under a pear-tree and wondered why his pulse raced so.

"What's the matter with me?" he murmured. "Am I going to be sick? Or am I just plain locoed by that moon? Well!"

He sighed, laughed softly at himself, and went on. He was in the shade now, but beyond him was a moonlit space where stood the little arched gateway in the hedge. He went toward it, his footsteps making scant sound on the soft turf; reached it; passed—but no, he didn't pass through just then. Instead he stopped suddenly, drew in his breath and stared wonderingly into the startled face confronting him.

XVI.

For a little time, perhaps as long as it took his heart to pound thrice in wild tumult, they confronted each other in silence. Then—"Eve!" he cried, softly; and—

"You!" she whispered.

Again a silence, in which he could have sworn that he heard his heart beating with gladness and the stars singing in the heavens.

"I—I wasn't sleepy," she said, breathlessly.

"Nor I. I didn't want to sleep. I wanted"—he stepped through the gateway and seized the hand that lay against her breast—"you."

"Please!" she cried, straining away at the length of her slender arm. "You mustn't! You got my note!"

"And tore it to fragments—an hour since! I don't remember a word of it!"

"But I meant it!"

"You didn't!"

"Let me go, please; I ought not to be here; I don't want to stay here."

"You must stay until—but you're trembling!" He dropped her hand and stood back contritely. "Have I scared you?"

"Yes.... I don't know.... Good night."

She turned, but didn't go. The moonlight enfolded her slim form with white radiance and danced in and out of her soft hair. Wade drew a deep breath.

"Will you listen a moment to me, please?" he asked, calmly.

She bowed her head without turning.

"You said in your note that you did not care to be made a convenience of. What did that mean, please?"

"You know!"

"But I don't. You must tell me."

"I don't wish to. Why do you try to pretend with me?" she asked with a flash of scorn.

"Pretend! Good Lord, is this pretense? What do you mean? Is it pretense to be so madly in love with you that—that yesterday and to-day have"— he caught himself up. "You must tell me," he said, quietly.

"I meant that I would not marry you to salve your conscience." She turned and faced him, her head back scornfully. "You thought some of that money should be mine and because I refused to take it you—you tried to trick me! You pretended you—cared for me. Don't I understand? You threatened one day to have your way, and you thought I was so—so simple that I wouldn't guess."

"You mean," he asked, incredulously, "that you think I want to marry you just so I can—can restore that money to you?"

"Yes," she answered, defiantly. But there was a wavering note in the word, as though she had begun to doubt. He was silent a moment. Then —

"But if I told you—convinced you that you were wrong? What then?"

There was no answer. She had turned her head away and stood as though poised for flight, one little clenched hand hanging at her side and gleaming like marble. He went toward her slowly across the few yards of turf. She heard him coming and began to tremble again. She wanted to run, but felt powerless to move. Then he was speaking to her and she felt his breath on her cheek.

"Eve, dear, such a thought never came to me. Won't you believe that, please? I care nothing about Ed's money. If you like I'll never touch a cent of it. All I want on this earth is just you."

His arms went around her. She never stirred, save for the tremors that shook her as a breeze shakes a reed.

"Am I frightening you still?" he whispered. "I don't want to do that. I only want to make you happy, dear, and, oh, I'd try very hard if you'd let me. Won't you, Eve?"

There was no answer. He held her very-lightly there with arms that ached to strain her close against his fast-beating heart. After a moment she asked, tremulously:

"You tore up—the note?"

"Yes," he answered. He felt a sigh quiver through her.

"I'm glad," she whispered.

Of a sudden she struggled free, pushing him away with her outstretched arms.

"You must stand there," she said, in laughing whispers. She crossed her hands, palms out, above her forehead to keep the moonlight from her eyes. "Now, sir, answer me truthfully. You didn't—do that, what I said?"

"No."

"And you won't say anything more about having your way?"

"No," he answered, with a happy laugh.

"And you won't ever even want it?"

"Never!"

"And you—like me?"

"Like you! I—"

"Wait! Stay just where you are, please, Mr. Herrick."

"Mr. Herrick?"

"Well,—I haven't learnt any other name."

"But you know it!"

"No," she fibbed, with a soft laugh. "Anyhow—well, so far you've passed the examination beautifully. Is there—is there anything more you have to say for yourself before sentence is passed?"

"Yes," he answered. "I came through the gate in the hedge." He went forward and dropped on his knee. "And I ask you to be my wife."

"Who told you?" she gasped, striving to recover the hand he had seized on.

"Miss Mullett."

"Traitress!" Then she laughed. "That was my secret. But I know yours."

"Mine? You mean—"

"Yes, about the name of your mine. I saw it on an envelope in the parlor the other night. I don't see why you didn't want me to know. I'm sure I think it was very sweet of Edward to name the mine after me." She looked down at him mischievously. He got to his feet, still holding her hands—he had captured both now—and looked down at them as they lay in his.

"It wasn't Ed who—I mean it wasn't exactly his idea," he said.

"You mean that it was yours?"

"Well, yes, it was."

"Indeed? But I suppose it was named after some one?"

"Ye-es."

"Another Evelyn, then," she said coldly.

"No—that is—well, only in a way."

"Let go of my hands, please."

"No."

"Very well. What was she like, this other Evelyn?"

"Like—like you, dearest."

"Oh, really!"

"Listen, Eve; do you remember once five years ago when a train stopped at the top of the Saddle Pass out in Colorado? There was a hot-box. It was twilight in the valleys, but up there it was still half daylight and half starlight. A little way off, in the shadow of the rocks, there was a camp-fire burning."

"Yes, I remember," she answered softly. "I thought we had been held up by train-robbers and I went out to the back platform to see. I didn't say anything to papa, because it might have scared him, you know."

"Of course," said Wade, with a smile.

"And so I went out and saw the track stretching back down the hill, with the starlight gleaming on the rails, and—"

"And the mountains in the west all purple against the sky."

"Yes. And there was a breeze blowing and it was chilly out there. So I was going back into the car when a dreadful-looking man appeared, oh, a —a fearsome-looking man, really!"

"Was he?" asked Wade, somewhat lamely.

"Oh, yes! And I thought, of course, he was a robber or a highwayman or something."

"And—he wasn't?" asked Wade, eagerly.

"No." She shook her head. "No, he was something much worse."

"Oh! What?"

"He was a deceiver, a—a Don Juan. He made love to me and made me promise never to forget him, and he promised to come and get me some day. That was five years ago. Why didn't you come?"

"Eve! Then—you knew? You've known all along?"

She fell to laughing, swaying away from him in the moonlight.

"Why didn't you tell me?" he asked, wonderingly.

"Why didn't you ask me? Yes, I knew from the moment I peeked in your window that day."

"Think of that! And I was sure you didn't remember at all. And now, after all that time, I've got you again, dear! It's wonderful!"

"Not so fast, please," she said, sternly. "You forgot me once—"

"I never forgot you."

"And you may do it again."

"I didn't forget you, dear. I still have that lilac you threw me. I—"

"You mean the one I dropped?" she asked, innocently.

"It was a week later that we found gold, Eve, and I named the mine for you. I worked hard that year, and—well, I'll be honest; I didn't forget you; you were always a sort of vision of loveliness in my memory; but—there was so much to do—and—"

"And you changed your mind. I see. And you never thought of poor me, waiting for you all these years!"

"I guess you forgot me quick enough," said Wade, ruefully. "When that other fellow came along, I mean."

"Stupid!" she whispered. "That was you."

"*Me?*"

"Yes, the you I met out there on the mountain, the you that made love to me and set my silly little girl's heart a-fluttering. Don't you think now it was wicked of you? Why, Wade—oh!"

"That's my name," he laughed.

"It's a funny name, isn't it?" she murmured, shyly.

"I suppose it is."

"But I like it. Oh, dear, I must go! It must be midnight!"

"No, only twenty minutes of," he answered, holding his watch to the light. "Don't go yet. There's so much I want to say!"

"To-morrow," she answered, smiling up at him. "Do you know that you're still holding my hands?"

"I don't know what I know," he answered, softly. "Only that I love you and that I'm the happiest man alive."

"Are you? Why?"

"Because you're going to marry me."

"I haven't said so," she objected.

"But you're going to?"

"To-morrow—perhaps."

"No, to-night—surely."

"To-morrow."

"To-night."

"Am I?" she sighed. "We-ell—do you want me to?"

"Yes," he answered, tremulously. He drew her to him, unresistingly. The moon made silver pools of her eyes. Her mouth, slightly parted, was like a crimson rosebud.

"Eve!" he whispered, hoarsely.

Her eyes closed and her head dropped happily back against his arm. The moonlight was gone now from her face.

Ages later—or was it only a few moments?—they were standing apart again, hands still linked, looking at each other across the little space of magic light.

"I must go now," she said softly. "Good night."

"Please, not yet!"

"But think of the time! Besides, it's quite—quite awful, anyway! Suppose Carrie heard of it!"

"Let her! You're mine, aren't you?"

"Good night."

"Aren't you?"

"Every little bit of me, dear, for ever and ever," she answered.

They said good night again a few minutes later and a little nearer the house. And again after that.

At a quarter to one Wade came to himself after a fashion at the end of the village street, smiling insanely at a white gate-post. With a happy sigh he turned homeward, his hands in his pockets, his head thrown back, and his lips pursed for a tune that forgot to come. A few steps brought him opposite the Doctor's house and the imp of mischief whispered in his ear. Wade laughed aloud. Then he crossed the street under the dark canopy of the elms and-pulled the office bell till it jangled wildly. A head came out of a window above.

"What's wanted?" asked the Doctor's sleepy voice. "Who is it?"

"It's Herrick. Come down, please."

After a moment the key turned and the Doctor, arrayed in a vast figured dressing-gown stood in the open door.

"Is it you?" he asked. "What's wrong? Who's ill"?"

"No one's ill, Doctor," said Herrick. "I just wanted to know if you had any remedy for happiness?"

Perhaps Wade's radiant, laughing face gave the Doctor his cue, for, after studying it a moment, he asked, with a chuckle:

"Have you tried marriage?"

"No, but I'm going to. Oh, I'm not crazy, Doctor. I was out for a stroll and thought I'd just drop by and tell you that I'd taken your advice and had decided not to leave to-morrow."

"Humph; nor the next day, either, I guess! Lad, is it all right? Have you seen her?"

"Yes, I've seen her and it's all right! Everything's all right! Look at this world, Doctor. Did you ever see a more beautiful one? For Heaven's sake reel off some poetry for me!"

"Go to bed," laughed the Doctor, "go to bed!"

"Bed!" scoffed Wade.

"H'm, you're right," said the Doctor. "Stay up and be mad as you can, my lad. Bay to the moon! Sing under her window! Act the happy fool! Lord, if I wasn't so old I'd come out and help you. Youth, youth! Now go away before I hate you for it!"

"You couldn't hate anything, you old fraud," laughed Wade. "Go back to bed if you won't sing or dance with me or recite verses. But first, congratulations, please."

"My dear fellow," said the Doctor as he clasped Wade's hand, "you don't need any one's good wishes, but I give mine just the same. It's good news to me, the best of news."

"Thanks, Doctor. Good night. I'm off to bay the moon."

"Good night, good night!"

The Doctor stood for a moment at the door and watched him pass across the strip of moonlight and become engulfed in the gloom of the elms.

"I wonder," he mused, "what he's done with his coat!" He chuckled as he closed the door, and sighed as he locked it. Then, instead of returning to the stairway, he passed into the study and walked across to the book-shelves. You would have thought that he would have had difficulty in finding What he wanted even in broad daylight in that confusion of volumes. But he put his hand at once on what he sought and bore it to the window where the moonlight shone. Bending closely, he turned the pages, paused and read half-aloud to the silent room:

"'Oh, love, first love, so full of hope and truth,
A guileless maiden and a gentle youth.
Through arches of wreathed rose they take their way,
He the fresh Morning, she the better May,
'Twixt jocund hearts and voices jubilant.
And unseen gods that guard on either hand,
And blissful tears, and tender smiles that fall
On her dear head—great summer over all!"

THE END.

Made in the USA
Lexington, KY
30 June 2017